TROY

BABYLON

ALEXANDRIA

SIDON

GIZA

THEBES

MEROE

TOPAZ
ISLAND

Chronicles of Ériu Series.

Volume 1 – The Demise of Affreidg.
Volume 2 – Cessair's Hegira.
Volume 3 – The Land of Plenty.
Volume 4 – The Fomorians.
Volume 5 – The Bronze Age.
Volume 6 – Tír na nÓg (Not published yet.)
Volume 7 – Partholon. (Not published yet.)

ISBN: 978-0-9956214-2-8

Published by Waring Estate Publication.
Email   publication@waringestate.com.
         Info@chroniclesoferiu.co.uk

Printed: Waring Estate Publications.

THE CHRONICLES OF ÉRIU.

VOLUME 2.
CESSAIR'S HEGIRA.

BY
MICHAEL H ST.C HARNETT

ILLUSTRATED BY KASEY LEITCH

The Chronicles of Ériu – Cessair's Hegira.

This book is dedicated to

The Brehons and Bards of ancient Ireland who, for many millennia, dedicated their lives to the memory of the Irish experience so that we may understand it today.

It is my great wish that their dedication is now recognised and appreciated as their interpretation of our shared history, rather than as just a fanciful rendering of myths and legends.

Glossary Volume Two.

Antonio – Sea trader from Santorini

Api – Mother Nature

Ardfear – Ceremonial name of supreme Scythian leader (Noe.)

Babylon – Ancient city many refugees fled to.

Balor – A Scythian became the leader of the Fomorian sea people.

Banba – Cessair's No.2

Bith – Cessair's father

Bridget – A Druid who joins Cessair

Capacirunt – Scythian master builder's settlement in Egypt.

Cessair – The heroine of this story

Dana – Cessair's best friend, a tribe leader, and a High Priestess.

Dûn na m-Barc – The fortress of the boats.

Farquhar – The pharaoh's keeper of the temples at Karnak

Fintan – Cessair's friend and confidante

Giza – Area of extensive building, later the site of the pyramids

Gomer – Dana's brother he later gives his name to the Gomerians

Grecius – Partholon's older brother and ruler of Thrace

Hatti – the leader of the Hittites

Hippolyte – The Amazonian Warrior Queen

Hittites – The followers of Hatti the empire builder

Kallisti – A Sardinian leader and trader

Ladra – Cessair's childhood friend, sea captain and shipbuilder

Matanni – A Scythian warrior.

Manandan – The sea god in the Endless Sea

Meroe – Cessair's island home in Egypt

Nel – Son of Scythian master builder and friend of Scotia

Nenual – Nel's brother and Pharaoh's intermediary for builders

Noe – Cessair's grandfather and leader of all Scythian tribes

Nubia – Area of Egypt that included Meroe

Nuralgi – A stone-built lookout tower

Phoenicians – People who specialised in international trading.

Partholon – A Scythian tribe leader and merchant

Saball – Cessair's foster father and later Pharaoh

Santorini – Island of expert metal workers

Sardinia – An island home of the Sherden

Scotia – Cessair's foster daughter, Saball's granddaughter.

Sherden – A tribe of Sea warriors from Sardinia

Sidon – The Phoenician city in Lebanon

Tabiti – The all-powerful Scythian god.

Thagimasidas – The Scythian god of the sea.

Thrace – Now Greece

Troy – Cessair's new town and port, named after her horse.

Lebor Gabála Érenn

Cessair, whence came she,
her three men and fifty with complexion?
A Tuesday she set firth, rough the story
From the islands of Meroe

.....

To the Torrian Sea without fear,
a-fleeing from the flood.
Three men, fifty tall maidens,
that was her tally with very rough fury:
a wind drave them, pleasant the fashion,
to Ireland a-wandering.

The Taking of Ireland. (Poems XXIII & XXIV)

Contents Volume 2.

Glossary Volume Two.	vi
Every long journey starts with a single step.	1
A tribe in despair	10
A place of their own.	21
The Greek connection.	25
The Egyptian connection.	33
New family ties.	48
Return to Affreidg	66
The time of changes.	78
Cessair's Hegira Resumes	86
The final push to 'The Land of Plenty.'	98
Postscript Volume Two.	104
Author's Synopsis of the Chronicles of Ériu Series.	106

Hippolyte

Every long journey starts with a single step.

Every long journey starts with a single step.

The morning after the party the night before is usually a relatively quiet time. A time to take stock and gently prepare for the coming day. The situation that Cessair and her tribe were in was anything but usual. Hippolyte was up before dawn as was her routine, but this morning there was no training for her, she was on full military alert, and this was now to be Cessair's 'Call to Arms.'

*"**Wake up, Cessair**. Things to do, places to go, and new country to find and tame."*

Cessair awoke with a start and jumped up, for she had been in a deep sleep and awoke from what seemed to have been a nightmare. She remembered the detail vividly; a god had attacked her country and submerged it under thousands of feet of water. She, young as she was, had been made the leader of a new tribe and had been tasked to go to the end of the world. Go to the Endless Sea to find and then occupy an unknown land. She looked around and thought,

"This is not my bed! What is Hippolyte doing here? Am I still dreaming?"

"Cessair! Are you awake?"

Hippolyte's words registered, and Cessair was awake; her faculties slowly registered themselves with her consciousness. It was not a dream, screamed her memory, but her rational thought insisted that it was all so weird that it must have been a dream. Hippolyte's presence, all 5'6" of her, standing right in front of her, in full battle gear, settled the internal argument in Cessair's mind and reality kicked in.

Cessair replied,

1

"Yes, I am now, Hippolyte, thank you. I am so pleased to see you here. Are you camped nearby?"

No chitchat from Hippolyte today. When Cessair thought about it, there was rarely any chitchat from her, and now that she is in operations mode, there will be none.

A short report of Hippolyte's actions followed smartly,

"Yes, I have secured a well-protected vantage point not far from here. I had Banba camp your tribe in our midst so we could give them maximum protection. I have already arranged for your share of the stock and food to be unloaded from the ark and brought up to your tribe. This is happening as we speak; it should be finished in an hour or so, and your horses are ready for you too."

Now fully awake, Cessair had to act as the new tribe leader and lead.

"Thank you, Hippolyte. I want to meet with you, Banba, Fintan, Ladra, my father Bith and Partholon, if he is around. If you have anyone in your tribe which should be there, please bring them along. I will tell my father, Fintan and Ladra if you can call the rest, please."

"Certainly, Cessair, I will prepare a quiet area in our camp, and we will be ready for you in one hour. At the latest, we must be on the move in a couple of hours. I will brief Banba and send her down to escort you to our camp."

This military urgency slightly unnerved Cessair but she knew that she was safe while Hippolyte's tribe of mounted warriors protected them.

2

Every long journey starts with a single step.

Bith was with his father Noe when Cessair found him. It was no easy task; whole tribes encamped for miles on either side. In total, tens of thousands of people had been part of the exodus from the ill-fated Affreidg. Hippolyte was right; they do need to move camp today. There were just too many people in too small an area.

Noe opened his arms as soon as he saw Cessair, and he ran up to her and held her tightly in a bear hug.

"My dear grandchild, Cessair, I am so proud of you; I am so excited for you. You have so much life to live and much to do with it. Go quickly now; you were right to enlist Hippolyte and her tribe's help. She is the best support that anyone can get, and you are so few. You are already a wise leader.

Keep me informed of your progress, and I will always send you what help I can. I will lead most of the tribes here to Babylon, and then we will split as I have directed. My name still carries considerable weight over an extensive area, so use it if you need to. Now, go quickly, I cannot stand goodbyes, and you need to be on your way. May Tabiti guide you and forever keep you safe."

It was Cessair who turned when Noe released his grip. She did not want to show her genuine emotions in case he thought her weak. Noe had no such hang-ups; he just watched his favourite granddaughter and youngest son leave him, probably forever. He had tears in his eyes as they went around the corner, but he knew for sure that he would permanently reside in their hearts as they would in his.

Around that corner, Cessair saw Banba. She was already waiting for them, and next to her were Ladra, Fintan, and even Partholon had been found; all were ready to climb up the slope to meet with Hippolyte.

Hippolyte saw them coming, and she beckoned them over to a quiet area for their summit. She pointed to a man Cessair had not seen since their childhood snow trip all those years ago.

Before Hippolyte could speak, Cessair spoke.

"Matanni, Great to see you; how are you? Seen any more giant tigers? Man, you look tough – how come you are here?"

"I am glad to see you too, and well done – your own tribe! Ardfear has put great trust in you."

Matanni was about to say something else, but Hippolyte cut him short by saying,

4

Every long journey starts with a single step.

"I have asked Matanni to join us because he has already scouted the way ahead, and he has a report for us."

Matanni suddenly became solemn and said,

"I have already checked out our route. There is a steep climb ahead, and with all the animals, it will take the rest of the day to reach the top. We will camp there tonight. From there onwards, the route is easy, and travellers frequently use it. It will take us another two days to reach the area we planned to go to. Many people from that area have left their homes since the ground shook, but that is not the main problem they face. They seem to be scared of attacks."

Hippolyte went on,

"So, the journey will not be too long or difficult, and there should not be too many threats on the way. To be safe, we will lead the way with my elite troops, and some of them will also take up the rear. I already have sent ahead scouts, who will stay hidden while watching out for ambushes or other threats. If there is no further business, we need to move."

Cessair spoke next.

"Thank you. You have prepared thoroughly, Hippolyte.

Partholon, you might have wondered why I asked you to come to this meeting when you have a large tribe of your own. I know you were planning to travel with Noe to Babylon and then look for your own place to settle and trade. Why don't you come with us, you can settle next to the new river that connects to the Black Sea, and when the sea is complete and level with the Sea of Marmara, you can travel by sea and trade with our tribes that remain around it."

Ladra continued, *"I have to restart my business so we can make boats big enough and strong enough to go safely to the Endless Sea. We could help each other to get started."*

Hippolyte joined in,

"With all of your people, we would have more people to defend, and we would not be such a burden on Cessair's tribe for growing

food. When Cessair moves on, which she will in a couple of years, you will have even more space."

Partholon was a little taken aback by this new opportunity and could see the benefits.

He then spoke. *"I will have to go back and discuss this with my family before I make any decisions."*

Hippolyte said, *"You must make up your mind quickly because we are ready to move now!"*

Partholon replied, *"Leave now, I will decide later, and I will send a message to you in your camp tonight. I wish you safe passage and be on your way."*

Partholon returned to his tribe, and everyone else readied to leave.

Cessair's horse, Troy, looked magnificent and regal when Hippolyte brought him over. Cessair was so pleased to be reunited with her 'friend' and keeper of all her innermost secrets. It had been months since she had been on any horse, but it was only seconds later that she had vaulted straight up onto his back and quietly spoke to him,

"Well, my old friend, another big adventure for us,"

and with that, they were ready to go.

She and Hippolyte led the column heading to their new lives. The exodus was over, they had finished running from, and now they were going to. Several times Cessair looked back, and she was humbled each time. She was struck by how many people were following her.

They reached the watershed at the highest point of their trail just before dark, and many were preparing to camp for the night.

Every long journey starts with a single step.

Fintan, who had now joined the lead party, said,

"If I drop this water here, it will drain back down the hill behind us, all the way back to Affreidg, but..."

He took one step forward,

"If I drop it here, it, like us, will go forward down the slope ahead of us and give new life."

He poured a few drops onto the ground; everyone did the same while making sure they dropped them on the right side of that very real and symbolic watershed.

The following day Cessair awoke early; it was still dark. She was sure she would be alone as she walked back over the watershed, waiting for Tabiti to give her light. There in the dark, she heard voices she knew; she called out,

"Ladra, Fintan is that you?"

"And me", came a reply from Hippolyte, *"and ...... Partholon is here as well."*

"Partholon! Are you coming with us?" The excitement was in Cessair's voice.

"Yes", was the reply. He went on. *"I have split our tribe into two, and most are following on behind. A small party will stay with Ladra's beached boat. If they can float it again, they will stay until it is safe to use it to travel, by the new sea, to Thrace, where Ladra lost his other boat."*

Ladra said, *"Do you always have to remind us of the boats I have lost!"*

Everyone laughed, and Partholon continued, *"With my tribe, we will have an extra three thousand people, and with Hippolyte's crack-mounted force and my foot soldiers, we will be capable of defending ourselves well from anyone."*

"There is the sun now, praise Tabiti," said Cessair, who had been watching closely, and everyone became silent.

It took a good few minutes before the full sun was visible. Everyone was quiet as they saw that all that remained of their beloved Affreidg was a vast black swirling sea.

Cessair stood up, walked well over the watershed, and called to her friends, *"Come, the view from here is so much better."*

She was right. Ahead of her, down a long gentle slope, was a new green and fertile land stretching almost as far as the eye could see. They were still relatively high up, and it was Ladra, who said,

"I can see the sea in the very great distance."

In less than a minute, the party's mood had changed from sombre to excitement and anticipation.

An hour later, they were again on their way after breakfast. Partholon joined the lead party, and they all made good progress that day. The sheer numbers meant that the line of people, animals and supplies stretched back for hours.

Now and again, they would come across a small settlement or travellers travelling in the opposite direction. Everyone they met on their journey had heard of the disaster that befell Affreidg, and they just wanted to help in any way they could. Some offered food and water or even just somewhere for a traveller to rest for a few minutes before resuming their hike.

They would need to camp early to allow the stragglers to catch up before dark. The scouts had chosen a defendable site, but it was in the hilly ground and the route wound its way between the hills, so the visibility ahead was poor. They reached the camp early to find Matanni patiently waiting for them; he had a worried look.

Hippolyte, Cessair and Partholon listened to Matanni.

"There is a huge camp of people just ahead of us, a ramshackle lot. They are distressed and look like they are running from something or someone. I do not see them as a threat, they have no soldiers or warriors, but we need to find out what the situation is ahead of us."

8

Every long journey starts with a single step.

Cessair said, *"They may need our help. I have to go and find out what their problem is."*

Hippolyte, ever cautious, said, *"I cannot risk you going alone. I will escort you with a dozen of my best troops and have a large contingent waiting in reserve not far away. We can keep you safe if things become difficult until we get support. Matanni, you come too, you have been observing them for a while now, and you must already have some knowledge of them."*

Most leaders, especially new ones like Cessair, would have avoided confrontation or even meeting with a large population of strangers. But Cessair was not *a typical* leader that focussed on working and benefitting only herself and her tribe. She cared and wanted to help all people, especially those in distress. The tribe *they were in made no difference; if they needed help, she* would do what she could.

"I am also coming with you." Said Partholon, and the small exploratory party were ready.

Once more, they mounted their horses, and a few minutes later, they rode off to help their neighbours in humanity.

A tribe in despair

They walked their horses around the next few corners so as not to appear too threatening, and they approached the camp, of many thousands, in a close formation of fifteen people. They expected some welcome or at least a group of their soldiers to approach them and ask them about their business. Instead, as they slowly made their way forward, everybody ran and hid; clearly, they were terrified.

A few seconds later, there was no one to be seen anywhere as they were all hiding. No one except a small child that had been forgotten, and he was sitting on the ground, crying. Cessair dismounted and went over to the child, and as she picked him up to comfort him, a woman came running out of her tent screaming. Hippolyte's entire troop had their bows out and pointing at the woman, but still, she came on screaming,

"Don't take my child. Please!"

Hippolyte raised her hand, and a dozen sets of fingers reduced the tension on their bows and the tension in the camp.

Cessair spoke quietly,

"I will not take your child. Why would you think such a thing? Come take your boy, and then please call your leader so I can speak with him."

The woman took the boy, fell to her knees and said, *"Thank you! I could not lose him like the rest of my family."*

With that, she left to go for her leader. Cessair looked around and saw a hundred pairs of eyes peeking out of everywhere; all looked terrified but still wanted to see what was happening. A few minutes later, she saw the same woman walking behind a young man who was obviously their leader.

A Tribe in Despair.

"My name is Hatti, and I am the leader of us miserable wretches. Please come to my humble tent so we can talk in private. We greet you as friends though we have seen very few of those in recent years. You are safe with us, for we have no fight left in us. Please come."

Hippolyte spoke briefly with one of her troops and then joined Cessair on the ground, as did Matanni and Partholon. They all walked with Hatti to his tent. There were now hundreds of faces with inquisitive eyes, all watching.

The tent was modest but well-appointed; this had been an important tribe with many rare artefacts on display. Something significant had happened, putting them into poverty and decline.

Hatti spoke and told them about his tribe. *"We were a prosperous and peaceful people; we had many animals and were learning to grow crops. Some of us were experimenting with building boats so we could also fish. We were all happy, we had many children, and our population rapidly grew. Then the ground shook, and our houses collapsed, and a few of us were killed, but we quickly started to rebuild. We were working day and night when the raids started. They came at night when the moon was round and bright. They attacked us in our sleep, killing many of our young men. They took our young women and many children away with them in their boats."*

Cessair and her friends listened in shock as they heard his story.

Hatti said, *"They just became bolder, and then they came in daylight with five or six ships. They rounded up our people like animal stock. Just yesterday, they came again and took the last of our young and this time, they enslaved many of our young women and men. Tomorrow, they will take them away in their boats to Thrace."*

"Thrace!" Partholon almost shouted, *"My brother has taken his tribe there. There is no way he would do that!"*

Hatti emphasised, *"They came from Thrace, ok. I don't think they were official somehow, no discipline, no honour; they were just out for themselves."*

Partholon was formulating a plan as he spoke, *"How many of them were there? How many of your people are captured and waiting to be moved?"*

Hatti replied, *"About fifty of them and five times that number of our people."*

Cessair looked at her friends, and she knew, just by looking, that they all agreed, so she said.

"We will help you, but we need to move very quickly. Do you have anyone who can ride and fight?"

"About fifteen, including me, that I could call on now. Not a great showing from a tribe of thousands!" Hatti said with a dejected sadness that was pitiful.

Hippolyte said, *"We will return in one hour, so be armed and ready to ride with us."*

Cessair's party left with such haste that all of the faces retreated, back into the shadows, leaving just visible the pairs of eyes; they were expecting the worst.

Less than one hour later, Cessair thought, *"If the eyes were hiding at the sight of a dozen armed soldiers, what would they be thinking now?"*

She was riding alongside Hippolyte, Matanni, and Partholon, and behind them were two hundred and fifty fully armed riders in full battle gear.

She expected to see no one, but instead, everyone was out. The excitement was palpable, and everyone was cheering as though they had already won; every one of those eyes now had hope in them. Hatti was there with dozens of willing volunteers; he looked splendid, and he carried a swagger that Cessair thought he must have lost months ago.

Hippolyte quickly inspected Hatti's troops; she was ruthless,

"You, you, and you, you are all too old and will hold us back. You, you, and you, you are too young and will also hold us back – we will teach you all to fight, in good time, if you want."

She looked at an ancient old woman who was barely able to sit on a horse not alone ride into battle,

"Honestly?" was all she said.

The old woman said, *"All I have in this world is my children and their families; they are corralled, boarded, and ready to be taken away forever."*

Cessair turned to a nearby woman and said,

"Look after this woman until we return."

Hatti and the remainder of his little army joined, and they all left at a fast canter.

It was dark as they approached the Thrace raiding party, which was to Hippolyte's advantage. She and Partholon had already worked on a plan of attack.

As expected, the raiders had sacked the small village closest to the boats, and they were drinking and celebrating their success. They never expected the Hittites to fight back, for they had already fled and were critically weakened and in total disarray. The hostages were already loaded, locked up within the ships, and guarded by only a few raiders.

In the dark of the night, Partholon and teams of his men would quietly board the ships. There was a full moon, so Hippolyte's best archers would watch from close by, ready to shoot any raider that might resist. The bulk of Hippolyte's troops would surround the village and hide. The following morning, Hippolyte's troops would attack them with overwhelming force when the raiders left to return to their boats.

The plan worked a treat, the most challenging part was capturing the boats, but with only the occasional struggle, the raiders knew they had no chance and surrendered quickly. Hatti greeted his people as they came off the boats and quietly whisked them away, under cover of darkness, to safety.

In the morning, the plan went even easier than expected. The raiders returned to their boats in twos and threes, and as soon as they were out of sight of the village, they were captured and locked away in one of their own boat's cells. The leader and about ten of his men were last to leave, and as they rounded the corner and caught sight of their boats, they knew there was a problem and immediately went for their weapons. Then they saw that they were surrounded and outnumbered, so they dropped their weapons and pleaded for their lives.

If Hippolyte had her way, she would have dispatched them all then and there. Her action would have acted as a deterrent to others wanting to raid in the future; it would have been much easier that way. There was, however, a bigger plan, so the prisoners were all brought down and locked up with the other raiders.

Cessair looked at the leader, and she recognised him despite him trying to hide.

"Balor! How could you? Why?"

was all she could say. She got no answer, and he skulked away again, only this time it was into a boat's cell.

A Tribe in Despair.

While the closest village to the port was badly damaged, the houses further out were intact. The place had been abandoned but not destroyed; it was just waiting for people.

Cessair called to Hatti and Partholon, *"Can we meet soon? We all need to talk. I have already asked Hippolyte and Matanni and sent messages to Bith, Ladra and Fintan to join us later."*

Hatti was a changed man, no longer the young, dejected excuse for a leader; he now carried himself at full stature and looked like he could take on the world.

"Come," he said, *"there is one place we can talk and have breakfast."*

His men, with the help of the freed tribe members, produced a fine meal, much to the surprise of Cessair.

"Now to business." Said Cessair, *"What are we going to do with Balor and his scoundrels?"*

Hippolyte and Hatti said they should make examples of them so that no one will challenge them again. Matanni, however, argued,

"If we just kill them, no one will ever know and think they had not just run away or were lost at sea. We now have 50 hostages, and I say we take them to Partholon's family in Thrace and negotiate with them for something we want."

Partholon continued, *"These men and their acts are an embarrassment to my family, and they will be made to pay. They will answer for their crimes over in Thrace and, what is more, by my brother Greecius. It will also show that we will no longer suffer raids from anyone and must be left in peace. We will take their boats as our own, as partial retribution for their crimes, but there will need to be more; much more!*

We will take them back to Thrace and let them be judged there."

Hippolyte offered some of her troops but apologised, saying they were not very good with boats! Matanni was keen to go with them to Thrace; unfinished business needed to be addressed.

Partholon continued, *"We will take five boats, crew them with my men and leave immediately. So that we will arrive in Thrace without being late and raising suspicion."*

Hatti then spoke, *"We have regained our dignity and many of our tribe who were being taken from us; I thank you all. If you stay with us, I will bring back the rest of my tribe and reclaim this land.*

A Tribe in Despair.

Partholon, please settle alongside us, around this sheltered port, and build your people here.

Hippolyte, I understand that you were also looking for your own land with your own rules. I suggest you settle in our land of Azzi. It is nearby. There is plenty of space, and it is good land for you to train; you may have it with my blessing. Furthermore, if you help protect us and train our new warriors, we will supply you with food and other domestic support to make you the best warriors in the world."

Both Partholon and Hippolyte agreed that they would be pleased to accept his offer. They thanked Hatti and said they still had a lot to do and would have to leave immediately.

Partholon and Matanni took about sixty of their best troops and boarded five of the six ships. Within the hour, they had left for Thrace. Partholon wanted to meet his brother; he had urgent issues to discuss!

Hippolyte also left with her warriors to ensure that all four tribes were brought across the country safely. Partholon's men that remained and the freed hostages helped to prepare for the arrival of so many weary refugees.

Hatti was left alone with Cessair as they looked around at the sacked village. He asked her.

"What are your plans, and what can I do to help you? You have given me the invaluable gifts of dignity and purpose, not to mention defeating my enemy and returning my country to me. You did this all with compassion and kindness. I will forever be in your debt."

Cessair replied, *"No one could have ignored the injustice set upon you. I hope you will help those who need it in the future."*

She went on, *"We are planning to move on across the seas to a new land in the Endless Sea. It will take us some time to prepare and build suitable boats. Please may we stay with you for that time? My father can show you how to grow more productive crops, and Fintan can show you the new metal he is making and ..."*

Hatti interrupted, *"Of course, consider this your home as long as you need it and not just as guests; take whatever lands you need. Of course, you do not have to show us your innovations unless you want to."*

Just as he was saying this, Cessair saw her father, Fintan and Ladra, walking up to greet them. She introduced them to Hatti, who then said,

"I have arranged temporary houses for you all. Please go and rest. You must be exhausted. We will all meet properly later."

And with those words, he left to greet his own tribe that was just starting to return.

Cessair went to join her tribe and was met with

"Hurrah." *"You have found us a great place to stay."* Said one, and another said,

"And great friends and allies."

Bith was happy because his crops could grow well there, and Fintan was delighted because there were plenty of exciting rocks from which to make metal.

Ladra said, *"A great port for boats, but the wrong type of trees to make ships capable of travelling over the Endless Sea."*

Banba was a little annoyed that she had missed out on the rout of the invaders, but she knew that the joining and moving of Cessair's tribe and Hatti's tribe was no easy job, and she had done it well. There was joy and celebrations, but they were very short because they all too quickly fell fast asleep.

First light, Cessair awoke and heard a few people. They were whispering while patiently waiting outside. When she went out, she saw the plucky grandmother that Hippolyte had rejected as a warrior. Behind her were two men, two women, and five children.

A Tribe in Despair.

"Meet my family. I have them again, thanks to you. We owe you everything and will forever do anything that you may need. Thank you, thank you!"

Said the old lady. Behind her was a basket piled high with the best foods they could get.

"Please enjoy this and call us when you need us for anything."

With yet another heartfelt *'Thank you,* they all left.

Ladra joined Cessair for breakfast and explained his problem about the lack of the correct type of trees. While he was talking about this, Hatti and Fintan walked past and saw the table of fresh food; a few seconds and pleasantries later, they also joined her for the lavish breakfast., Ladra was going into great detail about the type of tree that he needed when Hatti spoke,

"I know where you will find this type of tree. It is many days ride south of here in a country called Lebanon. They have great straight and strong trees called Cedars. I know the tribe there well; they have a funny nickname of 'Phoenicians.'

Go to a port town called Sidon. They will help you; they need a shipbuilder like you. I will send a few of my people to show you the way and help you."

Ladra was delighted and said, *"If you give me a few of your men, Fintan and I will take that spare ship and sail to Sidon. We will also take a few of our own people, and we can start to build big ships between us. I will also train them all to sail. It will take some time, but with this boat, we can always return and bring you to progress reports."*

Cessair asked, *"Do you know anything about these people?"*

"Yes!" Said Ladra, *"I have met them before, they are friendly enough, but they are very secretive. But they are outstanding businessmen, despite their funny name."*

Fintan added, *"Their name means 'The Purple People', or at least that's what Partholon's brother, Greecius called them when they went to trade with Thrace. They sell a valuable purple dye made from tiny seashells; they are covered in it and won't wash off!"*

Cessair, Ladra and Hatti all laughed while Fintan continued,

"Hatti, you have many of those shells around these shores; you should collect them and sell them to them. They are worth a lot to trade with."

Hatti then quipped, *"Then we too will become 'the purple people.'"*

Everyone laughed at that. Cessair smiled because she knew that Tabiti was working behind the scenes to help them.

A Place of their Own.

A place of their own.

A few days later, Ladra and Fintan were gone to Sidon, and the port was now empty. Hippolyte was moving her warriors to nearby Azzi, Partholon was still away with Matanni to negotiate with Greecius in Thrace, and Cessair found that she was at a loose end.

This was the first day since she had heard about the new deadly river in Affreidg, all those months ago, that nothing urgent needed her specifically. She could help her father, but Bith already had scores of people gathering crops or repairing fences, and she would only be in the way. Banba was organising her tribe and revelling in her organisational skills. She was giving orders to many, many people,

"Build this here. Here, there is great shelter. Put that there because it will be handy for water and ..."

Cessair hurried off, for she knew when to leave well alone. Today for the first time in many months, she could relax and how better to do that than to take Troy out for a long and leisurely ride? She needed time to be alone and think about the future. She decided to go west to see the Sea of Marmara that Ladra talked about when Thagimasidas threw the sea at the land and broke into Affreidg. She found herself getting cross at that name, and what he had done, so she spoke to Troy.

"There will be gods in our faraway land waiting for people to acknowledge them. I, too, will no longer recognise that nasty god, Thagimasidas, who destroyed Affreidg. All gods need us, people, to recognise them, or else they are nothing in this world. From now on, Troy, and in the future, our tribe will pray to the god 'Of the faraway land surrounded by sea.' I will call that god by using a word in our old language; 'Manandan.' A savage sea has always surrounded that god, so he is not threatened by it. I will praise Manandan; thank you, Tabiti. I know he is a good one of yours."

In a small way, she was happy with herself. She had rid herself of one evil god and enlisted another that had already proved to be up to the task.

Her thoughts turned to Hippolyte exploring Azzi, so now Troy was to hear all about Hippolyte,

"She is the mother of her new land, 'Mother of Azzi,' no, that does not sound right. I know, the old Scythian for mother was 'Am.' I will call her 'Am-azzi.' No, that's too harsh; 'Amazon' sounds much better. Hippolyte and her Amazonian Warriors – perfect!"

Cessair laughed out loud, but she was not quite sure if Troy saw the joke.

Time passed quickly, and she realised she was passing through lovely flat land perfect for farming. Just ahead was the point where the Mediterranean flowed into the Sea of Marmara, and that water would soon be flowing into the new 'Black Sea.' Now Troy was to hear why her tribe should move here.

"This place is perfect for our tribe because there is a good place for our boats. From here, we can travel to the remaining tribes in Affreidg, once the sea is full, or to Sidon, or for us to leave here bound for our new faraway land. Here is a great place to build our new town. Look, all the green fertile grass and freshwater you could ever need."

Troy gave a slightly muffled snuffle crossed with a whinny as though he understood that part. Cessair spoke again to her horse and confidante.

"You are now old; you have been my companion and friend; you have kept me alive so many times in all these years. I will name this new town that we will build here after you, and you can live out your days with all this grass and plenty of mares."

With those words, she turned around, and they started the long journey back.

A Place of their Own.

The duo had travelled very far that day, and a great many affairs of state had been spoken, but tiredness was not the most potent feeling uppermost in Cessair that evening. She now had a sense of calm; she just knew that things were going to sort themselves out and that she had just taken a tremendous mental and sensibly practical step on her hegira to find the new Affreidg. Her new town would be a necessary stepping stone to prepare her tribe for the next leg towards their destiny.

When she returned to Hatti's village, she called in with her father and asked someone to fetch Banba. Bith was just settling down to eat and was delighted to have good company to dine with him.

Halfway through the meal, Cessair casually spoke the words,

"I have decided to move the tribe again."

Bith and Banba just stared at each other in dumb amazement. Neither spoke because she was the leader, and her word was now law.

Bith spoke first, *"If you command it, then we will move; may I ask why?"*

Cessair replied, *"A fair and simple question, but I have to give you a vague and complex answer.*

The Hittites are different to us. They say they are peaceful, but I know that look in Hatti's eyes. When we captured Balor, he wanted more; he enjoyed the fight. When his tribe grows, he will want to take over new territories, not now, maybe, but in a few years. We must keep our social distance from our good allies and help each other but keep our core values pure. Hippolyte is doing just that by moving to Azzi, and I think we should do the same by moving to Troy."

Both Banba and Bith said together,

*"Move to your **horse**?"*

"**No!** *Don't be silly, that will be the name of our new town. It is in a great area, close to two seas, a freshwater river surrounded by flat grassland, ideal for your crops father. Hippolyte is close by if we ever need her help.*

Talking about names, I have a new title for Hippolyte; 'The Amazonian Queen and her Fearsome Warriors'."

At first, Banba and her father stared at Cessair after her words, but when she explained how she came to call her that name, they laughed and thought it suited her well. By the end of the meal, they all knew that this extra short move was not only necessary but also essential.

Hatti was slightly surprised by Cessair's decision but had no problems with it, and he wished her well; he even offered his tribe's help with moving them there. A couple of days later, Bith and Banba had taken an advance party to prepare for the move and a couple of weeks after that, Cessair's tribe had moved, and Troy had started to grow.

The Greek connection.

When they were well established in Troy, Cessair sent a messenger to Noe in Babylon. She wanted to know how he and the rest of the tribes were and to say that there was plenty of available land locally should another tribe wish to move close to her. When she was ready to move on to the Endless Sea, her new port town of Troy would also become available for them.

"I wonder how long it will take before I see that man again?"

She thought as she watched the messenger leave and about to disappear into the distance. A few minutes later, he was still there, and she thought he was coming back, but then she realised that someone else was coming to Troy. It wasn't many seconds after that when she thought,

"I know that horse and rider; Partholon, he's back. I wonder what happened in Thrace?"

In the time it took Partholon to reach Cessair, she had organised a welcome meal and fermented grape to be prepared. She called for Bith and Banba to join them.

She could tell that he had a difficult time because he looked aged, even in the short time that he was away.

"Good news and bad news."

Were Partholon's first words, he continued.

"We were able to bring back most of the Hittites that had been captured over the last few months, even most of the young children. That was the good news; for the not-so-good news, please wait for Hippolyte, I have already sent Matanni to Azzi to ask her to join us, and they should be here shortly."

Cessair raised a mug of fermented grapes and toasted the good news,

"To the safe return of Partholon, our people and to the Hittites – praise Tabiti."

She asked, *"Everyone did return safely; I hope they did?"*

"Yes!" Said Partholon,

"Everyone is back and celebrating with the Hittites. I am glad that only a few were injured and nothing serious. They are looking forward to coming here.

I came ahead to check if it is safe to bring the boats into your new port."

As he was speaking, Hippolyte and Matanni arrived and joined them at the table. Partholon looked around to check that no one else was within earshot; what he would say was only to be heard by the six in that room.

"When we arrived close to Thrace, we chose a tiny offshore island, unloaded all of the prisoners, and left them with water and food but no means of escape. We then sailed one boat straight into their main port, and I casually asked where I might find my brother."

Cessair asked, *"Was that not risky? They would have recognised the boats as Balor's."*

He continued, *"We figured that Balor's behaviour was so bad that he had to be doing it without the decent people of Thrace knowing and that he would have used unknown boats. We also thought he would not have used their port in the main town.*

We were right about Balor but wrong about my brother! The country is no longer called 'Thrace'. My brother has renamed it 'Greece,' after himself. The man's arrogance, I should have known what was to come next, but luckily, we were prepared for anything."

"What happened?" asked Hippolyte, *"Did you take your guard?"*

The Greek Connection.

"Yes, thankfully, but they were disguised as my friends! And Matanni had most of the warriors with him while he stayed with the boat and ferried supplies to the four boats left outside the port."

Cessair asked, *"But there was almost no one on those boats; why did they need supplies?"*

Hippolyte countered, *"The people in the town did not know that, and they just thought that the four empty boats were full of soldiers and that they were too dangerous or threatening to be brought into town."*

"Exactly, they were well fooled, they thought we had an army offshore, and the supplies would be needed later." Partholon continued,

"I went up with my small personal guard of friends to meet with Greecius and tell him about Balor and his acts. Greecius knew all about Balor and had even secretly given him money for each slave that he had captured.

*I had expected him to be horrified and angry with Balor. He became angry ok, but he got mad at me and ordered his small guard to arrest **me** – there and then!*

Fortunately, my warrior friends were armed and ready, and we took control of Greecius' room without killing anyone. Nor did anyone outside that room become aware of what happened within its walls."

There were audible gasps from around the table, and then he went on,

"I sat next to my brother at the table and pressed a dagger into his side. I then told him exactly what to say.

'Call out to your servants and tell them that we are your guests, and they will bring us food for a feast in my honour. Also, tell them that we are looking for some slaves that had been lost and that every slave, including the children, were to be brought to the port immediately.'"

"Did he comply?" asked Bith, shocked by the story so far.

"Yes, he did. There was one moment when he tried to say something else, but I just pressed the dagger a little harder, and he told them to leave the room and not disturb them for the rest of the night!"

Matanni took up the story.

"The main port is a little way from the town, in a different bay. My troops set up a checkpoint on the road outside of the port, heading into the town. When the slaves were brought to us, we said that we would take the slaves on ahead with us. We would identify them on board and that they would be collected in the morning, minus the ones we were looking for.

As the Hittites arrived, they realised it was a rescue, and they helped us by quickly boarding and carrying the small children. As each boat was packed, and I mean full, the ship sailed out of the port and was replaced by another empty one. All this happened under cover of darkness. This went on all night, and we were surprised at how many people had been taken over the last few months. Four boats were on their way home, and there were still plenty of Hittites to bring. We did not have room on the last ship, so we improvised and took the Greek boats. They were just sitting there empty, alongside the pier: we took three of them.

When the last boat was at the pier, and the last of the Hittites were boarded. We were starting to worry because the light was returning, and Partholon was not back."

Everyone sat in stunned silence, even Hippolyte, so Partholon continued with what happened in Greecius' palace.

"We pretended we were at a great feast, and we talked louder and louder. A few even sang and told jokes. To everyone outside the room, we were having a great family reunion, but inside, things were getting tenser by the minute. We quietened our voices close to the first light as though we were all falling asleep. We tied and gagged my brother and his people and left as if we had to return to our boat.

The Greek Connection.

We opened the doors to find a large, well-armed guard outside the door."

There were more gasps around the table, but no words were uttered, so he continued.

"I told the head guard that my brother had too much to drink, that he was in a foul mood and had just fallen asleep and that he must not be disturbed at any cost.

We quickly made our way down to the boat, and as we reached our men at the checkpoint, we heard an alarm being sounded. We ran as fast as our legs would carry us and boarded our boat, and left. A hail of arrows followed us, but we were already well out of range. Matanni had already disabled any of the remaining Greecius' boats, so they could not chase us."

"Wow, well done, how bravo…" the accolades just kept coming from the audience at that table, and they applauded Partholon and Matanni's bravery and ingenuity.

Banba was the first to say,

"We will have trouble with Greecius and Balor in the future," but they all knew it.

Partholon spoke again, *"Fishermen will soon find Balor as he is very close to the mainland. If he goes to Greecius, he will surely be killed after the shame of the whole incident and the loss of all the slaves. I bet that if Balor survives, he will move on somewhere far away from Greece.*

Greecius will become a problem, but he only knows about the Hittites and me. No one who saw Matanni would have known that he was with Hippolyte. So Cessair and Hippolyte, for the next year or so, your tribes will not be targeted as their enemy. However, the Hittites and I expect an attack in a few years when they have had time to prepare!"

Hippolyte stood up and said, *"Bring it on! We are ready already."*

Everyone else was a little more subdued. Until that is, Hippolyte was told of her new nickname. Everyone laughed, and Hippolyte did not quite know how to react, she did not like the ridicule, but she liked the name. She whispered, but still could be heard,

"The Amazon Queen and her fearsome warriors."

Everyone laughed even louder.

"Silence!" she ordered, *"**I am** the Amazonian Queen, and I do have fearsome warriors."*

She totally owned the title, and everyone stopped laughing; then she smiled a broad grin! And everyone, including Hippolyte, laughed heartily. Hippolyte was back to being almost human again.

The Greek Connection.

The next few days went quickly, and Cessair showed Partholon all around Troy. He inspected the port area very closely,

"Perfect he said; once again, you have chosen very wisely, Cessair."

The following year was hectic for everyone, between settling down and building up. The word about the daring rescue of all of the Hittites from the Greeks and of the protection of the now famous Amazonian warriors spread throughout the Middle East. People and tribes arrived from everywhere, and they all wanted to join in with the success of Hatti's large country.

Some of the tribes came in response to Cessair's message to Noe, and they, too, brought back a message from Noe for Cessair. Babylon did not work out well at all. There were too many peoples in too small an area. The Affreidgians from widely separated areas already had so many diverse languages that they hardly understood each other. Add so many new languages to the broad mix already in Babylon, the Assyrians, the Elam, and other countries; no one could even understand what their neighbours were saying.

The new society did not work, despite great civic works to try and bring together all the people and their gods. They even tried to build a massive tower to talk directly with the Gods, just as they did high up the mountain in Ardfear's Stronghold. This Tower of Babel and the wider society collapsed, and many of the tribes left to find new, less crowded homes in countries elsewhere.

Several tribes had moved to Cessair's area. Partholon's tribe already called their area Caria. It is in the southeast. They could see the importance of sea travel in the future, so they built several fine ports. The incoming tribes of Weshesh and Danuna settled around Troas, the name of the area around Troy. Others in areas further away became known as Mysia, Lydia and Phrygia. Other tribes leaving Babylon travelled southeast settling when they were happy. Some

Affreidgians travelled as far as Egypt and were given a new homeland there. The Pharoah gave the area in return for building.

All the tribes finding new homelands made Cessair feel slightly uncomfortable; she still had to find hers! Troy was prospering and starting to do well, but there was still no country where she could establish the old peaceful core values of Affreidg without undue corrupting influence from close neighbours.

The Egyptian connection.

One day there was great excitement, a real buzz around Troy, and the alarms sounded. Cessair heard them and thought,

"That is not the, we are under attack alarm. That is something exciting is happening. What can it be?"

Banba came rushing in, saying,

"Come quickly, look, it's huge!"

Cessair hurriedly followed Banba as she headed down to the port. Cessair looked around, and it appeared as if the whole of Troy was running down ahead of them. Cessair did not need to reach the port to see the cause of the excitement. It was huge, and it towered above anything else in the harbour. Cessair and Banba reached the pier just as the vast ship was tying up. The sides of the boat were so high that no one could see who was in the ship, nor did they even have ladders long enough to reach up to the deck. The next moment a rope ladder was thrown down from above, and someone started to climb down, and another person followed closely behind.

Cessair whooped with delight and shouted, *"I would recognise those backsides anywhere! Welcome home."*

Banba looked at Cessair with a puzzled look, so Cessair continued, *"It's Ladra and Fintan, of course."*

Then she welcomed the two with great hugs and kisses. Ladra spoke first, *"We have so much to tell you, but first, we have someone with us who hasn't seen you since you were a little girl."*

Cessair looked up and saw a behind she did not recognise, but she did recognise the old man as soon as he reached the ground and spoke.

"My favourite foster daughter, it has been a while. I am so pleased to see you all grown up!"

Cessair did not even get a chance to reply before Bith gave him a close embrace, which was normal between foster brothers. She turned to Banba, who had an even more puzzled look on her face.

"Go quickly and organise everything for our esteemed visitors. Prepare rooms and a meal fit for friends, family, and an ambassador! Oh! And call Hippolyte."

Turning back to her foster father, she heard Bith say,

"Seball, my oldest friend, what brings the Egyptian Ambassador to us this day? No, wait, come let us eat and catch up."

For a moment, he had forgotten that it was his daughter's position as tribe leader to make the invitation. Cessair knew that the excitement of meeting with his old friend explained his momentary lapse of decorum and that every other time that he had met Saball, he was the tribe leader, she said,

"Yes, of course! I have already arranged rooms for us. But first, father, please give Saball a brief tour of Troy and then meet us at my house in an hour."

"Thank you, Cessair. I will look forward to your company and to hearing your plans." Said Saball, and then Bith took him away through the crowd.

"Come with us." said Fintan to Cessair, *"Look at this great big ship that we have made."* Before he even had the words out of his mouth Cessair was climbing the rope ladder; both men enjoyed the view! Then they followed her.

The ship was huge, and the two men were very proud of their creation.

"It will carry four times more than any other vessel, anywhere." He said boldly and then, *"and it can carry heavy loads in the types of sea that we will meet in the Endless Sea. Unfortunately, we found*

that unladen, as she is now, the ship is hard to control and rolls dangerously in even light winds."

"So, always keep a load of rocks below deck as ballast and take them out when you have real cargo." Suggested Cessair. Fintan and Ladra looked at each other, and then after a long 'thinking' pause, Fintan said.

"Of course, we will…err… Do!"

Cessair laughed and then praised them on making such a great ship, and then she said,

"Come before we are late for our dinner. I am **meant** *to be the host!"*

Banba had organised everything perfectly. Cessair had learnt to expect nothing less from her. Banba couldn't help but ask,

"Saball is your foster father. What does that mean?"

Cessair explained.

"It is an excellent way to expand our family and make allies. Many years ago, the Pharaoh called Manual asked Noe to be a foster father to Saball, one of his sons. This forged a bond between the two countries as the families were joined and, therefore, unlikely to fight and more likely to help each other. Bith asked Saball, his foster brother, to become a foster father to me.

I am pleased to see him, but I wonder why he is here. Come, let us go in and find out."

When Cessair entered the room, Saball stood and immediately spoke.

"Cessair, I have heard so much about you over the last year, especially in the last hour, from your father. I could hardly believe that one so young, and a woman, could achieve so much so quickly. I have seen your new town, farms, metalworking, people, and even

allies; you are indeed a great leader and an excellent exemplar for them.

I had to come and see for myself if everything I had heard was true. From what I have already seen, you have surpassed even my expectations. As your foster father, Cessair, I salute you."

These words coming from one of the most powerful families in the known world made Cessair's face crimson red with embarrassment. This man, who would most likely be the next Pharaoh, praised her in her home. Cessair thanked Saball for his kind words, and they all sat down to a fine meal.

Cessair turned to Saball and said.

"With such an important international guest, I have invited my good friend and ally Hippolyte to join us and give us extra protection while you are here."

Saball replied, *"Thank you, my girl, I only brought a small guard on the boat, but I feel safe here among friends and family. I would very much like to meet this Hippolyte because her reputation has travelled widely like yours. I understand that most of her troops are women and are experts with the bow while on horseback."*

"She will be here soon, and then you will see the Amazonian queen and her fearsome warriors." Said Cessair, and most of the table let out a little laugh.

"Don't let Hippolyte hear that." Said Cessair just as Hippolyte entered the room and said,

"Don't let Hippolyte hear what?"

The Egyptian Connection.

Everyone laughed even louder, all except Hippolyte, who didn't get the joke. The meal went very well, but it was the camaraderie that was exceptional and relaxed and enjoyed by everyone.

Cessair was about to suggest showing her new guests to their rooms for the night when Saball again spoke,

"I am very good at judging people's character. I should be in my position. I wanted to spend a little time with you, to know you as an adult, before I ask you this next question.

Cessair, will you be a foster mother to my granddaughter Scotia? She will need a strong role model for her future."

The room went silent except for a few involuntary gasps and an *"Oh my!"* from Bith. To be asked to be the foster mother to perhaps the most important child on the planet made even Cessair lost for words. Then she uttered.

"Yes!"

Her eyes welled up, and her heart raced.

"I would be honoured and proud for my tribe, of course, and especially for me personally. Yes, I would love to be Scotia's foster mother."

She hugged Saball tightly. He was surprised and not used by such a personal display of affection, but he remembered the little girl of all those years ago, and he was no longer the Pharaoh's brother but a true foster father again, and he hugged her back as he quietly said into her ear,

"Don't tell them about this back in Egypt." In a louder voice, he continued,

"I am now sleepy, and a long sea journey makes an old man tired. I will go to my room and sleep well in the knowledge that 'The Fearsome Amazonian' has set up a guard outside. Thank you all, and good night."

All talked excitedly as Cessair showed Saball to his room and wished him a good night's sleep, and then she returned to the table. Everyone, talking at fifteen to the dozen, went silent and straining to see Cessair's reaction that should be written on her face. She tried to play it cool, but that only lasted a couple of seconds before her face exploded with a great smile tinged with pride. Everyone cheered and talked simultaneously, and then Bith quietened everyone and spoke directly to Cessair.

"You do know what this means, don't you?" He continued, not waiting for an answer. *"Remember that Saball came here a couple of times and spent a year or so each time to help with your critical education. Well, you must go to Egypt and do the same for Scotia."*

Cessair was silent, quietly processing, and everyone else also stayed quiet, trying to guess what she would say next. But they did not expect to hear the next words from her mouth.

"I am going to my room. Goodnight. Oh! Hippolyte, would you please walk me to my room."

The Egyptian Connection.

As they walked, she turned to Hippolyte and said, *"Please do not talk to anyone about my next question, even with my father.* **If** *I did go to Egypt, would you and your guard please come with me?"*

Hippolyte's reply was typical Hippolyte. *"I always wanted to try out an Egyptian Chariot; they are considered to be the most awesome weapon there is."*

Cessair smiled, and Hippolyte returned to the table, leaving Cessair to think quietly alone in her room. The seriousness of the situation became apparent when she realised that she wished that Troy was with her so that she could talk without judgement.

Hippolyte returned to the company, and no one even asked what they spoke about because they knew that Hippolyte would not say and because they already had a pretty good idea that everything was about to change again.

That night Cessair started overthinking about what she should do, and she found herself tossing and turning along with her thoughts that were doing the same thing in her mind. Then she remembered Ardfear's words while still at the top of the sacred mountain and before they boarded the ark.

"Truly ask yourself, don't push forward what outcome you think you want but just let it rise from deep within you, and you know it when it will be right."

Only a few seconds later, Cessair surprised herself and said out loud to an invisible horse,

"I will."

She then turned over, feeling content in her soul and peaceful in her mind. Then she promptly fell asleep and slept like a contented baby until the early morning.

Cessair, Banba and Hippolyte were all at the breakfast table, and there was not a single man in sight. Cessair took the chance and spoke,

"Banba, I need you to lead my tribe until I return. I will be taking my father and as many as will easily fill the ship. I need you to keep the majority of the tribe, which I will have to leave behind, safe and well. When we are ready to move on to the Endless Sea, I will return with more ships and pick you all up. Will you do that for me, please?"

"I am honoured that you have asked me, but I am so young and..." Said Banba, but even before she could finish, Hippolyte said,

"You are the same age as Cessair, and you have already taken care of the whole tribe, for many hundreds of miles, across challenging terrain and conditions – you are older than your years; of course, you can."

The woman she respected greatly and even feared a little encouraged Banba. She looked again at Cessair and quietly said,

"OK, I would love to. If you want me to."

"Great, thank you. I am sure that sometime in the future, we will be able to organise a trip for you to Egypt. We must have a good relationship with the Egyptians, especially when we go to our new island in the Endless Sea."

Banba smiled and said

"Thank you. I would like that."

When Saball arrived, he sat next to Cessair, and the other two girls politely left them alone. Saball spoke first, and his words surprised Cessair.

"I hope that I have not given you a poisoned chalice!

I know it is a great honour to be asked such a thing, but I have my motives, and it is only fair that you listen to them before you finally decide. You may well change your mind when you hear

everything. I only ask that you repeat this to no one, not even to your father."

Cessair agreed and then called out to Banba, who was close by.

"Please make sure that no one disturbs us until further notice."

Her attention, once more, returned to Saball as he continued,

"My brother is Pharaoh, and he has no children. I am next in line; it will be my son's role after me. I am worried about my brother; power has gone to his head. Fortunately, he is even older than me and is sick and may not last long. He is already making his sarcophagus and building his tomb as we speak. He is making it so large and grand; it just has to be much bigger than the rest.

The problem is that my son idolises him and hangs on his every word. I fear that power will also go to his head in time. I need Scotia to be influenced by a young, strong woman like you, for her sake and Egypt's. My son may well kill me to become Pharaoh, he is that power crazy, but he is still my son.

Watch yourself carefully if you do come, and do bring Hippolyte and her warriors as your personal guard with my authority and blessing. I will give you an island in the middle of the Nile, as this will grant you natural protection and also give you access directly to the Mediterranean if you should ever need it. Take your time, I have shown you the possible poison that may be in the chalice, but you have my word that no one, not even my natural son, will be allowed to put it there with my knowledge."

Cessair listened in amazement at her foster father's frank and uncompromising words; she knew from his sincerity that he was right. Cessair's next words surprised Saball and brought a smile to his face; they were.

"What is my new island home called?"

"Meroe."

Saball answered, and on his face, there was a broad grin.

The ship needed no ballast on its way to Egypt as it was packed with people and a larger-than-expected contingent of Hippolyte's warriors. *"To be sure, to be sure,"* was Hippolyte's comment when she heard she had a whole island to secure.

They stopped briefly in Sidon so Fintan and Ladra could see how the work on the other boats was coming along. All the leaders went ashore, but Hippolyte told her warriors to stay aboard as the sight of so many dangerous and armed women would have unsettled any city, and some incident or other would have been bound to occur. Only three of Hippolyte's and three of Saball's personal guards toured with the leaders as protectors for the day.

Ladra's new ships were progressing slowly, and the costs rose rapidly. Fintan said,

"Close to here, a black bituminous material was found oozing out of the ground. It is great for sealing the hull and keeping the water out. It must be applied hot as a liquid that sticks to everything and then goes hard as it cools. It is effective but expensive."

They were all shown a demonstration of how a basket of finely woven sticks hardly kept water in, but after treatment with the hot black liquid, it became as watertight as any flask.

Saball observed everything and then turned to Ladra and said,

"These are magnificent trees, much longer and straighter than any timber we have in Egypt."

"And stronger." Quipped Fintan.

Just one look from Saball sent Fintan scurrying away after his rude interruption.

"As I was saying," continued Saball, *"These long, straight, **and strong** trees would be great for our building works in Egypt. I will pay you handsomely for every tree you can arrange to bring to me in Egypt. Soon you will have enough money to build a fleet of ships if you want."*

The Egyptian Connection.

Ladra was delighted and quickly went to find the Phoenician traders who could carry trees to Egypt. He only had a few hours to agree on deals that would change not only his tribe's fortunes but also those of the entire Phoenician nation.

Cessair, Saball, Hippolyte and Fintan all approached their boat to hear a loud commotion on board. Everyone was on the deck or sitting on the cross masts. All were watching what was going on below and cheering or booing. They were all captivated by the spectacle. All except for a couple of Hippolyte's women, who then came over and started talking to her. Hippolyte was not pleased with such a sight in front of a party of tribe leaders and was about to go and stop proceedings when Saball turned to her and said,

"Wait! Let us see what happens; they are only practising spears."

Hippolyte explained that her troops were annoyed at Saball's elite guard calling them 'show troops', not real soldiers. So, they challenged their best six, against any six of them of their choice, to a spear and shield fight. They ridiculed the women, while the Egyptians chose whom they would make fools of. The battle started four hours ago, and neither side has won or lost any points, not alone ground.

Saball said

"This will do neither side any harm, and it will improve their respect for each other."

They whirled one way and then the next, but neither side got the upper hand. Saball added,

"Have they really been at it for four hours? Previously they have always cleaned up in only a few minutes."

Just as he said that, one of the onlookers shouted from the cross mast,

"You are in trouble now that your leaders are back."

That was all it took to break the impasse, the Egyptian troops only glanced across the deck at Saball, and their concentration was broken. Hippolyte gave a tiny smile while her troops took that crucial advantage, and the Egyptian best were finished off in the next few seconds.

The boat exploded with cheering and laughter and comments such as,

"Who are the show fighters now? Beaten by six random women!"

Hippolyte just raised her hand, and the whole noise and banter instantly stopped, and within seconds her whole troop were lined up in silence.

Saball addressed the whole ship,

"It takes a lot to beat my elite guard, as it has never happened before. Hippolyte, I am impressed by the discipline and focus of your troops; you have today proved to me that you genuinely are the Amazonian Fearsome Warriors.

When we return to Egypt, I will have my goldsmiths fashion you a golden weapons girdle in honour of today's impressive display. I sincerely hope our two sets of troops can learn much from each other in the future."

Everyone looked at Hippolyte, who gently nodded, and the ship was in an uproar again. Even the elite Saball guard recognised that they were beaten by not just women but by their warrior peers. So, they joined in as well, though in a much more subdued way.

A few days later, they saw Egypt and the town of Alexandria. It was the biggest town that Cessair had ever seen. It was nestled between two large rivers. They had reached Egypt, yet they still had a long way to go. As they entered the first river and passed the town, she asked Saball,

The Egyptian Connection.

"Which of those rivers is the Nile? They are both large rivers. I thought the Nile was the biggest river, yet they both look equally big to me."

Saball laughed and said, *"They both are and five more that are just as big."*

Cessair looked confused, so he continued, *"When a massive river reaches the sea, it is at the end of its life, and it slows down. It slows, and to let it live longer it brings land with it to extend its course. It also breaks up into little rivers to try and fool err, yes, I remember, you call her Api, so that it might look smaller and younger again. We have a name for when a river does this, and we call it a delta. We took that name because the river shape here is the same as that letter in your alphabet.*

See that building over there. That is the finest library in the world; you must see it soon. Bring Fintan; he would like it too."

The river they were sailing on was large, but after an hour or so, another larger river joined them and then another and another and yet another. The combined river was now huge, and they kept heading inland. As they passed one monument or building after another, there was a constant utterance of

"Oohhs" or *"Ahhs"*

from all of the visitors, including Fintan, who was usually above such facile comments.

"We are now passing Giza." Said Saball, *"We are planning to build some huge monuments here. To help us, Noe sent some of your tribes. In return for their help, we have given them fertile lands they may call their own. They call their lands Capacirunt."*

The Nile journey was to last days before they would reach Meroe Island. Cessair's new home, for a while. They had stopped briefly in Thebes while Saball confirmed that everything was ready for him, Cessair, and her escort. From there, two much smaller boats followed them to Meroe, but they always kept a respectful distance behind. When Meroe was in sight, Saball said,

"This is the Nubian region; you will like them. You have a lot in common. We also know this area as 'Ta-Seti' or 'The Land of the Bow,' they claim to be the best in the world."

Cessair was glad that Hippolyte did not hear that last point, as it would have put her in a bad mood.

Meroe was a large island, and everything about it was large, the houses, the stores, and the buildings. It even had a palace, and everything had been prepared for their arrival. Cessair was the leader of a tribe, but this place was fit for a queen of a nation. No sooner than they had landed than Saball said,

"This is your new home, and as a 'daughter' of mine, anything you need will be immediately brought to you. If it is not, or you are not happy, send me a message, and I will deal with it, and they will never repeat the mistake."

Something was chilling in how he spoke those words that made Cessair slightly uneasy. He went on,

"I am leaving a boat for your use, for when Ladra leaves with the big ship. In five days, I will send a boat for you to bring you back to my palace in Thebes so that you may meet Scotia."

A few moments later, he had boarded the smaller river boat and he and his men were gone.

Fintan and Ladra looked around, at each other, and then at Cessair. Ladra spoke first,

"This place is huge, and it has everything. People are offering to do things for us everywhere we go, all trying so hard to help us. It would be so easy to sit back and do nothing; everywhere we look, tall black Nubian women are assigned here to help us with everything. Fintan, we are heavily outnumbered here!"

Cessair laughed and said, *"Aren't you sad that you will be travelling so much and will not be able to enjoy the luxury? Fintan, you, on the other hand, need to learn as much as you can from these people, they are so different, and their importance is growing rapidly. We could learn so much from them."*

Hippolyte joined them; she was not happy and rhymed a list of problems,

"Too many people we don't know on this island. It is too big to easily secure, and I don't want these local women doing everything for my troops; they will make them 'soft!'"

Cessair thought that it was the third point that worried Hippolyte the most. She said,

"We do not need so many of these people to look after us. Send most of them home permanently and the rest every night. Hippolyte, keep an eye on the pier and see just who is coming and going."

"I already am."

Was her prompt reply.

The next few days were about finding their way around and seeing so many new things. Ladra found that the Nubians traded extensively with the countries to the east. A short trip across land brought them to the Red Sea, and the boats from there travelled to many exciting new countries. Fintan found out that the Nubians mined many metals here, including gold. Most of their metals and imported eastern materials sales went to Thebes. Cessair then realised why Nubia was so important to the Pharaohs.

New family ties.

A fine boat arrived at the pier and docked on the agreed day. Shortly afterwards, angry shouting could be heard over a large area of Meroe.

Cessair was walking down alone to meet the visitors when the commotion started. She arrived at the pier, along with many others, to see what the problem was. She was amazed to see an official-looking gentleman and his armed escort surrounded by Hippolyte's troops. He was red in the face and very angry at being detained.

Even as Cessair approached, she was circled by Hippolyte's troops, this time in a protective formation. Cessair turned to one of them and asked,

"What is happening here?"

The warrior explained, and Cessair then said,

"Warriors, please stand down; these people are guests."

The human rings immediately dissolved, and Cessair knew she had a diplomatic incident on her hands. She tactfully spoke,

"Sir, I am so sorry for the inconvenience. The warriors were only following my instructions: no one was to enter the island without my knowledge."

The man was no happier and almost spluttered out the following words.

"I will not be stopped from going anywhere I want, and definitely not by a few women. I will have them all flogged for this."

Cessair was annoyed and spoke in a very firm voice,

"Sir! You will not speak to me in that tone of voice…"

48

She saw all the warriors were again on full alert and weapons readied but not fully raised. She continued,

"I will not have my warriors abused for following my instructions. Please return to my foster father Saball and ..."

She stopped mid-sentence as all the visitors had dropped to the ground in abeyance. They had not recognised who she was. They were used to throwing their rank and power around without being challenged. Cessair composed herself and then spoke softly,

"Gentlemen, please stand. We have started very badly, and I apologise for my part. Warriors, please go to my house and have them prepare a welcome for these people. Sir, please accompany me alone so we can become properly acquainted before meeting anyone else."

With those words, the man told his guard to wait for him at the pier. They waited, but with considerable surprise as they never usually left him. He spoke nervously,

"My name is Farquhar. I am so sorry; I had no idea who you were. I was completely out of line."

The tension was almost gone, but the diplomatic incident was far from gone. He went on,

"I am the keeper of The Royal Karnak complex in Thebes. Within it, there is a palace where Scotia is kept."

Cessair did not like the choice of words that he used or the implications they conveyed. She thought she would change the subject,

"Please let me introduce Fintan, and we will have some light refreshments."

Farquhar seemed to relax with Fintan, and Cessair resolved to leave them at the first opportunity after they started their refreshments, all in the name of diplomacy. Her chance came, and she spoke with Hippolyte about what really happened earlier.

"He refused to wait at the pier, and he told his guards to kill mine if they would not let him pass!"

Said Hippolyte, *"That is a man who is used to having everything done his way."*

Cessair praised her guards' actions and agreed with Hippolyte that weakness should never be shown to bullies.

"I will need a small guard for my trip to Thebes."

"I have them ready. I want to meet this Farquhar!" Replied Hippolyte.

Cessair cringed slightly at the thought of Hippolyte's diplomacy, but she also thought that Farquhar deserved the introduction.

The incident was over, but certainly not forgotten. Everyone was polite when they boarded the boat, and each had its designated place. The central cabin area was for the dignitaries, the front for Hippolyte's troops, and the back for Farquhar's. The boatmen seemed to be everywhere and anywhere, not least the tiller man who stood mainly on the roof.

Cessair watched the river, the countryside, and the people. Ladra watched the boats, piers, and trading posts. Fintan watched the buildings and temples while Hippolyte sought out the sentry posts and barracks. Both sets of guards just watched each other and sent taunts and gestures when they thought the dignitaries weren't watching.

The boatmen just wanted to arrive as quickly as possible and safely; they feared that anything outside the boat was safer than the tensions inside, and that included the crocodiles that swam in the river around them!

Thebes was impressive. It looked grand from Ladra's boat but now they were standing on its royal pier just in front of Saball's palace. Cessair thought,

"That is nice of Saball to come down to meet us. Why is everyone so surprised to see him here? Why is everyone almost cowering back? Even Farquhar?"

"Welcome, daughter; please bring all of your party, including your guard, into the palace. I know this is highly unusual, but I wish to demonstrate to everyone the respect I have for you, and that will stamp your authority on them."

Cessair replied. *"Thank you for bringing us into your magnificent palace, but my guard would best stay here, just inside the hall."*

Saball took Cessair by the arm and signalled the others to wait. They walked alone through Saball's palace into an extensive and private garden area, past a couple of temples and then they reached another much smaller but still impressively large palace.

"This is Scotia's palace; she has lived here for all of her life." Saball sighed and continued.

"Her mother died in childbirth, and her father had no interest in his wife or daughter. I chose her name as a mark of respect for your Scythian peoples; in Egypt, a person's true name is especially sacred and vital that it is often kept secret.

My son has no time for her, he sees her as a nuisance, and she is just an inconvenience to him! I keep her in Thebes because I fear what might happen to her if she were not living in my Palace complex. He tolerates her because he now thinks that perhaps sometime in the future, he may be able to make a deal with some neighbouring country and then marry her off to some prince as part of the deal."

Those words saddened Cessair, but she asked.

"Has she spent all of her life here? Where does she learn? Where are her friends? What sort of life does she have?"

"Oh, she has had nannies and tutors from before she could talk. The best of everything as far as things are concerned, but she has had no life as a child! I doubt her father would even recognise her now. I can't remember when he last saw her; a good few years ago, I think.

I see her whenever I can, and I do enjoy our visits; she reminds me so much of my dead wife. She has the same enthusiastic view of life and joy in simple things, and she always wants to see the best in people. The problem is that I am so busy, and my visits with her must be kept short. As an ambassador, I have to travel to many local countries, which takes a great deal of time."

Cessair noted the guard outside the door when she followed Saball inside. They walked through the dark passages, up a broad staircase, and entered a large but dark room. The walls all around were covered with brightly painted pictures, but the colours failed to show their true beauty as the room was only lit by small reed wicks that gave off a feeble light.

The whole place was quiet save for the echoes of their footsteps. There were no other sounds of life throughout the building. No sounds of children playing, no sounds of people working, cooking, singing, no sounds of everyday life at all.

Saball called out, her name reverberating around the great room and through the dark and distant corridors.

"Scotia!"

Silence, then a faint and distant reply followed by the sound of light footsteps running. Faintly at first, they seemed to be coming from far above them, and then they got louder and louder.

A young girl burst into the room and ran straight past Cessair, who was standing in the shadows, and she continued running until she leapt into Saball's waiting arms. Cessair so clearly remembered herself doing exactly the same thing to the same man not that many years before.

"Oh! Grandfather, you came to see me. I am so glad to see you too. I was on the roof watching the outside world. There is so much out there; I want to see it all."

Scotia then saw Cessair and immediately jumped back as though she had been caught doing something terrible.

"I am so sorry."

Saball spoke next, *"This is my foster daughter Cessair. Come over and meet her properly. I hope that you will become good friends."*

Scotia came over very shyly and said.

"I have had many tutors and servants, but I have never been allowed to have a friend. It is very nice to meet you."

Cessair was taken aback and felt very sad for this polite little girl who had spent so much of her life alone yet was still so full of life. Cessair asked.

"You are very pretty. How old are you?"

"Thank you, I am ten." was her reply. *"Would you like to see around my house?"*

"Very much," said Cessair.

Saball said, *"Go ahead, you two. I will return in an hour."*

From the rooftop to the basement, Scotia took Cessair everywhere around her large palace. But with every room, Cessair realised just how much of a prison poor Scotia was in.

Scotia asked,

"Why do you have such a big tooth around your neck?"

"There are two of them. I will tell you a story about two best friends and how each of them got a tooth from a great big tiger!"

Cessair sat down, and the little girl eagerly sat close to her and examined the tooth. Scotia listened intently to the story of a group of young friends who had gone searching for snow. How they camped by the river and climbed the tallest mountains, all to find this white stuff they had been told about by their elders. She explained how a colossal, savage and frightening tiger had attacked the party. She squealed when Cessair gave a loud ***Roar*** mimicking the noise of the tiger.

"Who were the girls?" Asked Scotia.

Cessair slowly replied, *"Well, Dana was one and..."*

"You were the other."

Shouted Scotia in excitement.

"I want to go on a trip like that; it sounded like such fun."

When Saball returned, Cessair turned to Scotia and said,

"I will try never to have to ask this of you ever again, but this once, I need to speak to your grandfather alone."

Cessair did not want to raise her hopes only to possibly have them dashed if Saball disagreed with what she knew she had to say to him.

Scotia's head dropped,

"Of course, I enjoyed having you as a friend, and I liked your story. Goodbye."

She left a shadow of the happy little girl who first came bounding into the room.

It was Saball's turn to look surprised when Cessair started to ask a series of questions.

"Scotia has lived here all her life, and nobody other than very trusted servants knows what she looks like?"

Saball nodded in agreement.

"You want me to be Scotia's foster mother?"

Saball nodded again, and Cessair took a big breath before continuing.

"Ladra has several years to establish his supply line to Egypt and prepare our fleet for the endless sea."

Yet again, Saball nodded in agreement. There was no expression on his face, so she continued after taking another big breath.

"Scotia needs to come with me to Meroe!"

Silence…. followed by a long pause. Her heart was beating rapidly, and the only noise that she heard. Then Saball powerfully said,

*"**This** is Scotia's home; **this** is **my** home."*

The tone implied that this was the end of the matter. Cessair knew that tone, and throughout her life, she would never have spoken back, but this time, it was the right thing to do.

In a respectful but firm voice, she said,

*"**My** home is Meroe, and a daughter should be **with** her mother in **her** home."*

Silence, followed by more silence. Saball's face became slightly redder. He had never been spoken back to before in this manner. Then his reasoning came back to him, and he said with an accepting tone,

New Family Ties.

"I wanted a strong woman for Scotia. You are exactly what she needs; you were even prepared to displease me to help Scotia. Nobody should displease me."

Then there was another long pause. His face changed as a broad smile developed.

"She may go with you to Meroe!"

A little shriek was heard above them.

"Yes!"

Saball laughed and then called out,

"Will the little eavesdropper please come down and join us? Now!"

The rapid little footsteps from a distance returned, but this time when she burst into the room, much to Saball's surprise, it was Cessair whom she hugged.

Saball continued, *"Nobody outside my immediate palace knows either of you. To everyone, Scotia will be your daughter, and that is to be our secret. This palace will be maintained as though she were here and officially in residence."*

Cessair explained about the incident with Farquhar as this could have repercussions for Scotia. Saball laughed out loud, then said

"He is a very loyal man, but he can be very arrogant sometimes. I will speak to him if you want..."

"No!" Cried Cessair,

"That was not why I told you. He just assumed he had the right to barge into my home without invitation. If he thinks that, so will others."

"I see." Said Saball. *"I will declare Meroe as an independent country and an ally that is under your control. No one will risk an incident by entering without invitation and authority from you.*

Come now, Scotia, prepare yourself, my granddaughter. You are about to meet the world with your new mother."

Cessair offered Scotia her hand. This show of affection was new to Scotia, who held it timidly at first until they reached the front door. Then Scotia gripped her as though her life depended on it; in many ways, it did.

Saball led the way through the gardens, past the temples and back through the palace. Scotia held back somewhat timidly until Cessair gently squeezed her hand and said,

"Walk proudly beside me, daughter."

Scotia stepped up, straightened her back and said the words for the first time in her life.

"Yes, Mother!"

There was a great big smile on the little girl's face, and Cessair felt a heartstring being pulled beneath her breast.

The rest of the visit to Thebes was a blur. Everybody was stunned at what was happening, but they all knew better than to ask or say anything. Cessair turned to Saball and said.

"I think it best that we return quickly to Meroe and, if we may return soon, to visit you and to see Thebes. Next time, Scotia and Bith will also come."

Saball smiled and agreed,

"I can't remember the last time I have been manipulated by anyone other than my dear wife, but I believe it is also a daughter's prerogative. Take great care, you two. You are my closest family now that my wife has died, and my son only cares about himself."

On the trip back to Meroe, Ladra watched the boats and piers, Hippolyte watched the sentry posts and barracks, Fintan watched the buildings and the temples, and the two sets of warriors watched each other, still with the occasional taunt. Farquhar watched nothing; he just wanted to leave them all off and return to Thebes. Cessair watched Scotia, and Scotia watched everyone and everything.

Bith returned from an expedition to look at plants from further up the Nile. He was happy to meet Scotia, and she was delighted to have another grandfather figure in her life. The only practical restriction on her was that she should not leave the island without the company of Cessair, Bith, Fintan, Ladra or Hippolyte. Any approved visitor was allowed onto the island as long as they checked in and out at the pier.

Scotia's tutors had educated her well in theoretical subjects but very poorly in practical life skills. It had been assumed that her life was to be little more than a suitable marriage to some foreign country's leader and that she would always have servants to do everything for her. Her education was now Scythian style, and the best person for the subject taught her; she had to learn about all aspects of life. Bith for animal husbandry and growing crops, Fintan for the more formal topics and Hippolyte for self-defence and the theory of warfare. Cessair took her wherever she went, and the two learned about real Egypt together.

They learnt the difference between the Egyptian Gods and the Scythian ones. They all had different names, but both sets of gods crafted the world out of chaos. The big difference between the two sets was that the Scythians believed that the people and gods continued to craft the living world together and that the gods were everywhere in the trees, the water, and the sky. The Egyptians, however, believed that the gods had finished all the work of crafting the world and that people needed to thank them for it continually.

The Egyptian gods were worshipped as idols, such as statues in temples, rather than intangible Scythian deities living in seas or forests. Scotia learnt the importance of belief to any people and its significance as a thread in the fabric of society that helped keep it all together.

Astrology was a new subject for Cessair, so she took lessons along with Scotia and learned about it together. Ladra had shown Cessair which stars helped him to navigate boats at night, but astrology offered them the insight of the gods as to the direction that a person's life would take. They learned how the stars moved in a strictly choreographed dance to the tune of god's will and how those movements affected everyone and everything. Everywhere there were lines of divine force passing through the physical universe. They learned how to use tools, such as pendulums, to manifest these force lines that permeated the material world. The best pendulums were made of Topaz and came from an island in the Red Sea.

The most important lesson of all was one that Cessair had already learnt at a young age: to respect Api and work with her. Her friend Dana had dedicated her life to this subject that she and Scotia were scratching the surface of. Cessair missed her friend and her insight into the divine.

They met Bridget, who was from one of the Scythian tribes working in Giza. She, like Dana, was studying the power of the gods and was particularly good at it. They spent many hours together learning how to interpret the movements of pendulums and how these simple instruments could annunciate the gods' will.

Cessair was frequently invited to public events as an honoured guest, and Scotia accompanied her as her daughter every time.

Cessair was worried that Scotia was too old to learn to ride correctly, as usually Scythians were sat on horseback as soon as they could sit up. Cessair taught her the basics on a carefully selected quiet horse, and a few days later, Scotia was hooked for life! Within a few months, whenever they travelled anywhere, if there was an option of horse riding, she would take it.

A few years passed very quickly for Cessair, and Scotia was becoming a strong independent young woman. Saball was forever lavishing great gifts upon his two 'girls' and organising all sorts of events.

For Scotia's thirteenth birthday, a wild animal party was organised. This was a lavish event, with guests transported in specially made cabins on the backs of elephants. Cessair and Scotia enjoyed the spectacle of these animals, but they enjoyed the spectacle of Hippolyte's face even more, when she first saw them.

The same day, they watched Hippolyte ride a camel for the first time. It was a bad-tempered animal, but it still kneeled on command for its rider to mount it. As soon as Hippolyte mounted its back, it turned its head and looked at Hippolyte straight in the eye so that its face was only a couple of inches from hers. It then let out an almighty sneeze.

New Family Ties.

While Scotia and Cessair were laughing, and Hippolyte was crossly wiping her face, the bad-tempered beast stood up with such speed and force that the hapless rider was catapulted into the air and was lucky to land back in the saddle.

Scotia collapsed in convulsions with laughter, and anyone watching her just had to laugh as well. The giant camel was still not satisfied, and it promptly took umbrage and galloped off into the distance with its very competent, angry, but nevertheless powerless rider on his back. The whole party fell about laughing at the sight of the errant camel disappearing with a veritable posse of horse riders galloping behind it to try and catch it up.

A few months later, Saball's brother died, and Saball was made Pharaoh. There was one ceremony after another for the rest of the year, and each was more impressive than the one before. Impressive as they were, both Cessair and Scotia soon became jaded, and they even started to tire of them.

One day as they were on horseback riding along the Nile, Cessair turned to Scotia and said,

"You are now fourteen, and in Scythian society, you soon would be ready for your 'selection.' You will be an adult on your next birthday, and my role as your guardian will be over."

Scotia turned quickly and anxiously asked,

"Will that mean you will no longer be my mother?"

"No, silly, we are now tied to each other forever."

Cessair paused and then continued,

"I will be leaving Meroe soon; I must continue and find the island in the Endless Sea. Some months ago, Ladra finished building the ships we need, and now that they are ready, it will soon be time for us to move on."

There were tears in Scotia's eyes when she said,

"I can't go, can I?"

"No, Scotia, you are needed here for the next few years. When you are older, I hope you will visit me."

Cessair continued, *"I have one big journey to make, back up to Troy and around my former country. It is now mostly the Black Sea, but we still have a few settlements around its coast. I need to plan for my tribe's big move, and I want one last look around."*

"Can I go with you on that trip?" Asked Scotia somewhat wistfully; she was fully expecting a no.

"If your grandfather allows you to leave the country," said Cessair, *"I will ask him. I do think that the experience abroad would be good for you.*

I had planned not to return to Meroe after my trip back to Troy and around Affreidg, but if your grandfather allows you to come, I could always return to Meroe to bring you back. I could then get the last of my people at that stage."

Scotia's mood definitely lifted with the possibility of going with her foster mother on their own private adventure.

64

Saball had complete trust in Cessair, but it still took a little 'daughter' persuasion for him to let Scotia go.

Cessair explained that their trip would take a few months and that, at its end, she would not move back to Meroe. She would instead continue her quest, her hegira to the Endless Sea.

Saball was greatly saddened but acknowledged that Cessair had *performed* her foster mother duties exceptionally well. She had carried them out so well that he could not refuse her anything. *Because of that,* Scotia would be allowed to go with her.

When Scotia heard the good news that she was allowed to travel with Cessair, she let out an excited.

"Yes!"

Cessair's mind instantly *returned* to the *excitement and enthusiasm expressed by that same* monosyllable word that Scotia shrieked when she first learned that she could leave the palace and move to Meroe all those years earlier.

Scotia had grown, matured, and transformed into a well-rounded person. *She was* confident in her wider world and, most importantly, confident in herself. But despite all of her changes, she never lost her enthusiasm or joie de vivre.

Despite the heartbreak of the separation that would inevitably happen soon, Cessair knew that Scotia was now ready for the next adult phase of her life.

Return to Affreidg

There were a great number of preparations to be made before Cessair could leave Meroe. Most people on Meroe would be leaving forever. Five years is more than enough time to create emotional and physical ties, so there were mixed emotions in Meroe while they were preparing to leave.

Cessair called for Scotia and asked her to walk with her. She had to talk about a very serious matter.

"When we return from our trip," she started,

"I will not be staying on Meroe. It will be difficult to leave, so I will not make it any more difficult. I will pick up any remaining tribe members that do not want to stay and live here, and then I will immediately leave to join up with the other ships in Troy.

You still have your childhood palace in Thebes, and magnificent it is. I worry, however, that you may need space that is truly your own, especially if something bad were to happen to your grandfather. I am giving Meroe to you. Your grandfather gave it the status of a country so you can have a safe place of your own, with your own troops that will solely be loyal to you. Hippolyte has been training a new guard of local Nubians for you, and she says they are turning out very well. You probably saw them around recently."

Scotia, the bright, vivacious and vocal girl was speechless, there were so many conflicting emotions, and she really could not express them; she just hugged her mother and cried.

There was great excitement when Ladra's big ship once more entered the Nile and sailed up to Meroe. It stopped off in Giza to unload its cargo from Sidon so that the now lighter vessel could more easily travel upriver. A few days later, it made its way back down, but this time it was loaded with Cessair's people.

As they were sailing downriver now and again, people were offering camels at the riverbank. This was most peculiar, and crewmembers started asking what was going on. Scotia, Cessair and Fintan just laughed. Some idiot was foolish enough to ask Hippolyte, but she stormed off, saying she did not like boats or camels.

They stopped off at Thebes, and Saball wished them a safe trip and gifted them some luxurious supplies. They also briefly stopped at Giza as the ex-Affreidgian tribe leader Nenual had a big request to ask of Cessair. He asked,

"I was born in Affreidg over thirty years ago. I am the son of Feinius, our tribe leader. When I was young, we moved to Babylon as master builders. We started to build the great tower there, but then, the then Pharaoh invited us to bring our skills here. He gave us this land and pays us well to build great monuments for him. This is working well for us. I am their leader, fluent in so many languages that I was put in overall charge, and I report directly to the Pharaoh.

There are now several more tribes here, and there are a few from each tribe who do not like Egypt and want to go with you to find the new Affreidg."

Cessair agreed but requested that each tribe represented had a nominal tribe mother and father to act as tribe representatives. The next time that she would pass, when returning to Meroe, they would have only a few days' warning, and they had to be ready to leave.

She was just about to leave when Nenual asked Cessair for one more favour,

"My little brother Nel has been visiting me. He loves it here but needs to return to Babylon, where he was born, and our father and his mother are still living. If you could bring him to Sidon, there are people there who will take him the rest of the way."

Cessair replied, *"We can certainly take him, but it will be weeks before we reach Sidon as we are going to the Black Sea first. He looks so young. How old is he?"*

"Only fifteen; our father remarried in Babylon. He has to stay there, as he is the leader of many tribes in a huge area. They lived close to the great new tower still being built. That allowed us to meet so many different people from everywhere while they were working on it. Meeting so many diverse peoples led to us learning so many different languages."

Nenual continued,

"Nel loves to travel. He wants to see where all those different peoples came from; it would be a good experience for him. He is forever talking about your expedition to the Endless Sea."

Cessair smiled and said, *"In that case, how can I refuse? What is more, he will be good company for Scotia."*

As the ship passed Alexandria, an excited Scotia said,

"This is the furthest I have ever been. Fintan used to take me to the library there, but we never went any further."

Minutes later,

"Is that the sea?

Are those sea waves?"

She was a little girl again but it was Nel, an equally excited young man, who answered her questions this time.

The journey north was uneventful, but the prevailing wind was against them, so it took two days longer than expected. Nel was keen to learn all about boats and was constantly asking questions of Ladra. But for most of the trip, Cessair noticed that he and Scotia were rarely apart.

Return to Affreidg.

Troy was in sight, and everyone was on deck as the ship approached the port. Cessair had been telling Scotia about Troy and how it was a tiny village around the harbour. Troy was no longer a small village. As far as she could see, there were new buildings and people everywhere. As the ship was drawing up to the pier, Cessair turned to Scotia and Nel, saying,

"When this boat first docked, it was so large that everyone had to climb up and down on a rope ladder; it was very undignified. They now have a much larger pier for Ladra's ships."

She was about to continue when a cheery voice called out,

"Welcome home. It is so good to see you. You are looking so well."

Banba was standing there with a great beaming smile across her face.

"There have been so many changes. Let me show them to you. I am sure you are all tired after your long journey. It is already late, so we will leave the tour until tomorrow morning."

Banba then saw Scotia and Nel just as Cessair said,

"This is my foster daughter Scotia, and I would also like to introduce you to Nel."

"I have heard rumours about you, Scotia, and they are all true. You are truly beautiful."

Banba replied, and Scotia blushed slightly; Banba went on to tease,

*"Is this **your** young man?"*

Both Scotia and Nel now went bright red, and both cried out,

"No!"

Cessair and the others close by laughed at the young ones' expense.

"Sorry, Scotia and Nel, I did not mean to embarrass you, but you look so well together." Apologised Banba.

"It's all right, Banba, but we are just friends." Said Scotia. She looked at Nel's face and then added,

"Very good friends."

Return to Affreidg.

Cessair's first question for Banba, as they were walking up to her house, was,

"Who are all these new people, and what do they want?"

"Babylon did not work out very well." Replied Banba. *"Too many people in too small an area. Many tribes left after the new Babel tower fell. The tower and their hopes for a new future in Babylon fell together; they said both were stretched too far. There are now dozens of tribes who want to go to the Endless Sea to find a new home with you! Fortunately, there is plenty of space near Troy. Many are now encamped and settling all the way up the coast."*

"Oh!" replied Cessair. That was all she could say, as she had not considered this a possibility.

"We will need to talk about this soon. Maybe later at my home. Is everything ok at home and in Troy?"

"Yes, and everything is ready for you. All I have to arrange is a room for our new guest, Nel."

With those words, Banba hurried off to do a little more organising. Her parting words were,

"Partholon will call by tomorrow morning."

"This is my home in Troy, and I am glad you and Nel can see it. It has changed so much since I was last here, and so many new people have come into the area; I hardly recognise it." Said Cessair.

"It is lovely," replied Scotia, *"and so much cooler than Meroe; I love it."*

"I am not surprised that the Babel Tower fell!" Said Nel, *"There were so many different groups of people working on it with no overall plan. A set of builders would build a few levels then a new*

71

team would take over for the next level. The many different teams spoke different languages, so each new team had no idea how the lower levels were built, and there was always a team willing to take the risk of adding just one more level to the building."

"There is a lesson for us all to learn from that Babel tower." Said Cessair, *"We must not overstretch our capabilities."*

"Do you mind if Nel and I go and explore Troy?" Asked Scotia.

"Find Banba first and see if there are any places to avoid. There are so many new people here that I know nothing about." Was Cessair's cautious reply.

Scotia and Nel were gone in a flash!

Cessair sat back in a comfortable chair and just relaxed. This was the first time in many days that the floor beneath her did not move in sympathy with the river or sea.

Banba returned with two chalices of fermented grape, sat down alongside Cessair, and spoke.

"I am so pleased that you are back. You have been away a very long time, and so much has changed. The Black River no longer flows, and the waters rise no more in Affreidg. Many tribes have settled around the coast of the new Black Sea, and we have started trading routes with many of them."

Just then, Bith, Fintan and Ladra, who had seen the comfortable chairs and fermented grape, thought they too could relax, and they joined them.

Banba continued, *"With the disaster in Babylon, the tribes have further split. Some travel down to Egypt to help with the building boom and join Nel's brother in Giza. Many of the metalworking tribes came here, and Partholon helped them to settle here, and he moved others on to Cyprus, Rhodes, and Crete. Very few places have* the right type of rock, so those tribes move to where the rock is. If they are close to the sea, they can sell their metal to many more people by sending it by boat. They can make so many things from this new copper, which is much easier to find than gold."

"That is great news!" Said Cessair.

"It is", replied Banba, "but there are still so many tribes looking for new homes; over forty of them! Most of them want to come with us!"

"Forty!" was echoed by the seated audience.

Cessair voiced everyone's concern; "There is no way we can cope with so many tribes, and it would be too great a risk for all to set off into the Endless Sea. A few tribes, maybe, but no more!"

Bith now stated the next problem; "If we reduce the number of tribes, we are hurting most of our original people who will have to stay behind with nowhere to go. If we take them all, we put everyone at too great a risk."

"We do not have enough boats for them all." Added Ladra.

Fintan's contribution to the discussion was, "We need enough people to set up a few settlements of a manageable size and find out what we can make there."

The relaxing atmosphere had gone, and Cessair now had another problem. Cessair then said that Partholon would join them in the morning and that they would sort out the route forward without the clouded judgement offered by the fermented grape. The men left, and Cessair and Banba were alone again, talking about anything and everything. They were just about to go to their beds when Scotia and Nel arrived. Nel spoke first:

"We love Troy; it is so young and vibrant, with so much opportunity. I am so glad I had the chance to see it. I can now tell my friends that they should also come here."

"Thank you, Nel; your words have helped me more than you can imagine. You have just solved a big problem that I was facing.

Now let us all sleep, it is late, and we have a lot to do tomorrow. It is even more important now, that we move very quickly."

With those words, Cessair left, and they all went to their beds.

The new day brought a new sense of urgency. Cessair now saw the path forward, thanks to Nel's words the night before. She saw the next step and a clear way to the foreseeable future. Breakfast was over; Partholon had arrived, as had Banba, Hippolyte, Bith, Ladra and Fintan.

Cessair took clear command of the meeting and started with a series of questions to each person present. From Ladra, she found that there were about eighteen ships capable of the journey and that they could only take a small fraction of the people who wanted to go. From Bith and Hippolyte, the ideal tribe size for food production and defence from wild animals. From Partholon, though, she asked the most questions; about the metalworking tribes that went to the Mediterranean islands. Cessair then spoke as the tribe leader to everyone at once.

"We cannot take everyone, but in a sense, we will."

Everyone looked at each other confused then she continued.

"The three original tribes will first travel and settle in three different areas. That will take twelve ships; the remaining six will take representatives from each tribe that wants to come. From each extra tribe, two men and two women will join the three new settlements and become part of them. They will then, after some time, return here to their original tribes and advise if they too should travel to the new country."

74

Return to Affreidg.

This solution seemed to satisfy everyone, but before anyone could speak, Cessair continued.

"Tomorrow, I leave for a trip around the new Black Sea. I plan to stop at many new settlements and repeat this message. Two months from today, all the ships loaded with people and supplies will assemble here in Troy. We will then all leave together for our new home in the Endless Sea."

Everyone could feel the excitement in that room, and it was not many minutes later that the excitement spread throughout Troy and beyond.

It did not take long for Ladra's ship to cross the Sea of Marmara, but Ladra recognised very little as they approached what used to be the northern coast. There he had seen the small chasm. He could almost have jumped over, but now the chasm was so wide he could hardly see the beach on either side. The last time he was here, he was on horseback!

There was only a gentle current as he sailed ahead, and after a while, there was the vast Black Sea ahead of him. Everyone was silent and thinking about that terrifying exodus with the ark those all too-few years ago. Now it was just sea, for as far as their eyes could see, drowning their beloved Affreidg.

It was Scotia who spoke first.

"Are those the mountains where you killed the tiger?"

Her keen eyes had spotted, far to the west, the outline of a mountain range. Cessair immediately grabbed for the tooth around her neck; she remembered and wondered about Dana.

"Yes, possibly. I can't tell anymore. Ladra, can we head in that direction?"

As the boat approached the coast, they saw the River Danube, and Ladra navigated up it a short distance. They saw a large settlement just ahead. Cessair almost shrieked.

"That is the bend where we camped alone. Now it is a large town."

A large crowd met them at the pier to welcome them. The news of Cessair's return from Egypt was well known, as was Cessair's proposed trip around the Black Sea coast. This surprised the travellers; they were learning that news now travelled very fast indeed.

Cessair learned that the leader with the great teeth marked on her arm had moved on many years earlier. The story of the great tiger was now folk law and told to all of the children. She heard that Dana had left them, saying she had the promise to fulfil and was travelling upriver to the west. No one saw the small tear welling up in Cessair's eye, but Scotia did ask,

"Mother, are you ok?"

There were many stops on their circuit, and the whole experience was bittersweet. It was great to see old friends, but the entire trip was ruined by the memory of what was lost.

For Scotia and Nel, the Black Sea trip was just that. They did not experience what had happened before. Looking at that vast sea, it was hard to imagine what now lay below. It was an exciting holiday for them, but now that they had returned to Troy, it would only be a matter of days before they would be separated when Nel would have to travel back to Babylon. They both lost much of their youthful exuberance and became inseparable. Cessair started worrying about Scotia because soon she, too, would leave her daughter alone in Meroe. They were all in a sombre mood when they entered Cessair's home and were greeted by her father.

Return to Affreidg.

"Welcome home; you must tell me all about your trip. But first, I have an important message for you, Nel. You are to return to Egypt and not go back to Babylon and that your brother will explain everything to…"

The shrieks of joy from both Scotia and Nel drowned out the rest of Bith's words.

"Scotia and Nel, both of you go out until you settle down. That is no way to behave."

Cessair sternly reprimanded them, but simultaneously, a huge weight was taken from her heart. The two were quiet, but only for the time it took to rush to the door without running. Once outside, they made so much noise that they never heard the laughter of the people they had just left. The duo would not be back for a long time.

Bith continued.

"He is to return to Giza as several more of his father's tribes are joining Nenual, and his father will also go there in time. So many tribes are abandoning Babylon, there are major problems out there."

"I am so pleased that Scotia will have a close friend in Egypt even if he is at the other end of the country. It will make my leaving so much easier."

Said Cessair as she almost fell back into her comfortable chair.

She could sit back and enjoy her evening without worries for the first time in a long time.

The time of changes.

By not having to go back through Sidon to leave off Nel, they would save a couple of days and would now sail straight to Giza. The following day everyone in the area was busy preparing for the next great move of the tribes. Cessair felt confident enough to take Scotia and Nel to visit Hippolyte and her tribe in Azzi.

Troy, Cessair's lifelong horse, had died while Cessair was in Egypt. He had been retired with a herd of fine mares, and almost every foal born since then showed the same promise Troy had as a foal. The oldest of his foals was now old enough to be ridden, so Cessair chose him for the ride to Hippolyte. Scotia also chose one of Troy's foals because she particularly liked the look of his head and Nel said,

"Just give me something safe; I am not a very good rider!"

Cessair chose a large and heavy-working horse that was close to retirement. Nel looked at the tall mare and said,

"It is the tallest of them all and the furthest to fall to the ground. Can I have a tiny one?"

Scotia laughed when she comforted him by telling him,

"She may be big and tall, but she will be safe and much easier to ride. Furthermore, she will not shy or jump at the sight of a bird or animal that may scare her."

Nel needed a lot of help to mount the mare's back, but once there, he soon gained confidence and was ready to go. It did not take long for him to relax enough to start a casual conversation.

The Time of Changes.

"I only ever really rode bad-tempered donkeys or bouncy little ponies. I have lived in towns for most of my life and never really needed to learn."

"You will need to learn before visiting me in Meroe. We will even take camels into the desert." Said Scotia.

Nel winced, and Cessair laughed.

Hippolyte had organised a great day for the trio, everything from fine food to military demonstrations to a very impressive master class in horsemanship. Cessair thanked all those who had spent so many years with her in Meroe, and all were sad when they mounted up to ride back to Troy.

On their ride out of Azzi, they had to travel through a long pass with high ridges on either side. It was a tremendous defensive feature, and it was one of the reasons that Hippolyte had chosen this large valley in Azzi as her home base.

"Look!" said Scotia, who saw them first,

"The whole tribe is lined up on both sides, giving you a guard of honour. This is more impressive than anything I have ever seen in Egypt."

The entire Amazonian warrior army assembled would strike terror in any adversary, but instead, Cessair was in tears because she knew just how great that honour was. It was only performed once or twice in a generation and then only for great Amazonian leaders. The last warrior on the right, also in full dress, was Hippolyte. She looked magnificent, and she even wore her now-famous golden girdle. She had a great smile on her face as Cessair passed.

Cessair was just about to shout up, but before she had time to open her mouth, Hippolyte raised her hand, and the entire army disappeared as one. The ridge was instantly empty and silent; the whole experience was now only a treasured memory in all of the trio's minds.

The ship's passage back to Giza seemed to pass in a flash. The winds were with them, and the sea was calm enough for fast travel. Even the passage up the Nile was quicker than the last time. Nenual was alerted of the imminent arrival of Ladra's ship and was already on the pier to meet it.

"Welcome back, Cessair, Scotia and you too, Ladra."

Nenual then saw Nel,

"What are you doing here?"

The change of plans was explained to him, and he appeared to be delighted that his brother was staying as he 'really was quite useful to have around!' In brother speak, that was indeed high praise.

Cessair then explained the policy of first taking only four from each tribe to travel to the Endless Sea.

"For those Egyptian tribes who are unhappy to stay here for the next few years, there is space for them to spend that time around Troy or in Cyprus. I will take the representatives with me when I pass here again, in a few days, on my way back down the Nile."

With all of the business concluded, a somewhat dejected Nel stood on the riverbank with his brother while Scotia sat alone at the front of the boat. Cessair then sat at the front with her and said,

"Have you not already agreed to meet in a few weeks? He is now living in the same country and ..."

"Stop the boat!"

Shouted Scotia. Cessair thought that she was overreacting to leaving Nel.

*"Stop the boat. **Now!**"*

The Time of Changes.

The second cry with authority from Scotia put people into action and the man who was letting the mooring rope slip through his hands quickly grabbed it and retied the boat. It stopped with a jolt causing a couple of people to fall over.

"What is wrong?"

Shouted an angry Ladra.

"Listen!"

Said Scotia. Everyone became silent. Nothing was heard, and Scotia called,

"Wait!"

A baby's cry was heard from the front, and many crowded the deck to see where the cry came from.

"There in that basket made of rushes." Shouted Scotia.

In seconds the baby and the life raft of a cot were on the deck next to Scotia. She said

"Who could have abandoned this child and yet loved him enough to protect him so well from the river? I will bring him with me to Meroe, and he will have a chance of living a life."

A few minutes later, the ship was once again sailing up the Nile.

The stop at Meroe was brief. Most of the tribe that was leaving were already packed and ready to board. Many had decided to stay in Meroe with Scotia; they had already made many local ties and enjoyed Nubian life. Scotia had many families on Meroe only too willing to raise the Baby of the Rushes, and one of them quickly whisked him away to a warm feed and a comfortable cot.

The dreaded goodbye was on the brink of being said when the Pharaoh's impressive barge was spotted approaching. Ladra's ship was already loaded and just waiting for Cessair, but he knew he had to clear the pier for the Pharaoh.

Cessair quietly spoke to Scotia, she said.

"You are now the owner of Meroe; it is your duty to welcome the Pharaoh officially."

Scotia performed her duties flawlessly, and the Pharaoh appreciated the importance of the symbolism. Once they were safely inside and in private, Saball became the loving grandfather and foster father that they both loved. He turned to Cessair and said,

"Send Ladra on ahead to Giza. I want to spend a few days with you two before you leave Egypt. I will very slowly bring you two down to Giza on the Royal Barge."

Cessair knew that part of the reason for such a generous gesture was to ease the pain of the impending goodbye. As though he was reading her thoughts, Saball continued,

"I hope that you, Scotia, will stay a while with me in Thebes. You can, of course, return here to Meroe any time that you may wish it."

Cessair knew that Saball would keep Scotia so occupied that she would have little time to miss her.

The trip back down the Nile was splendid, and even Saball acknowledged that many of the onlookers were there to see the departure of the leader who brought those famous Amazonian warriors. They spent most of the first day talking about their recent trip back to Troy and on to Affreidg. It was inevitable that Nel would be mentioned at some stage, and Saball even started to tease Scotia about him, and each time she would blush. Even Cessair was surprised by what Saball said next.

"When we return to Thebes, after Giza, I am going to publicly introduce you to Egypt as my granddaughter whom everybody believed was living secretly in my palace."

He turned to Cessair,

"Egypt is forever in your debt for what you have done for her, but I am sorry to say that, as per our agreement, they can never know officially!"

Cessair's reply was simple but honest,

"I got by far the better part of our agreement, and my life has been greatly enhanced by it."

Before everyone became tearful, Saball again shocked, this time by saying,

"When we get to Giza, I want to meet this Nel. I know his brother Nenual. He is the joined tribe's representative, a competent man. Maybe Cessair, you would introduce me to your young trip companion when we are there."

Cessair replied,

"I will, of course. He is an admirable young man."

There were huge crowds at the piers at Giza, and all work had temporally stopped for Cessair's departure and the royal visit. Ladra's ship was already loaded and ready to go awaiting its solitary remaining passenger.

Cessair and Scotia were to accompany the Pharaoh on a quick official tour of the new building works. Nenual was summoned from the crowd but was surprised to hear that Nel was also required to attend. Ladra, fortunately, had thought such a summons was a possibility and suggested that Nel looked his best. The introductions were over; the small party toured the construction site. At the end of the tour, Saball thanked the brothers for their attendance and dismissed them. Back on board in his private quarters, Saball said,

"Nel is a fine young man, and you may bring him to Thebes to see me at any time."

Scotia gave Saball a great hug, just as she had done all those years ago when Cessair first saw her. Cessair saw the initial shock on Saball's face then the grandfather's love took over once again. He extended an arm out the Cessair to join them; this he had never done before. Not a word was spoken for a long time by any of them, and then it was time to go. There were no suitable words that any of them could say, so Cessair, once again, just turned and left.

The Time of Changes.

There were loud cheers as she boarded her boat, but Cessair heard nothing as she climbed on board. As soon as her foot touched the deck, Ladra cast off the mooring ropes, the sails were already up, and Ladra's ship started rapidly moving away. She looked back at the royal barge to see Saball and Scotia waving from a private deck and consoling each other. Fintan put a comforting arm around Cessair, and she buried her face in his chest and wept.

Four days later, they were back in Troy.

Cessair's Hegira Resumes

Troy was packed with ships, people and supplies, all ready to load up and go. Cessair arrived to find that Banba had achieved near administrative perfection, and most practical decisions had already been made and acted upon. Cessair was in no mood to hang around, and she was sure that everyone else felt the same.

There were some final meetings that she had to hold before they left. They were with the three separate tribe leaders, Partholon, Hatti and Matanni. Banba had already set them up, and everyone was assembled.

Matanni, who was initially in Dana's tribe and had moved to Hippolyte's for the exodus, had left Hippolyte's tribe and had created a new one, taking members from many different tribes but still associating and allied closely with Hatti's. Cessair's earlier concerns were well justified; Hatti and Matanni had become obsessed with creating an empire. Cessair tactfully asked how their tribes were doing, and Hatti started to fill in their story.

"When you first left for Egypt, we thought we would return to farming, which is what we started doing. Fintan and Ladra had talked so much about those Phoenicians traders and those shells that we gathered them and sold them. It paid us well, much better than farming. Then with the arrival of some metalworking tribes from Babylon, we found that we could make so much more money by producing metal.

One of the trading vessels said that there was a much better rock for the metal in Cyprus, so Matanni took and established a tribe there. They pay us handsomely every month, and then Matanni brought another tribe to Crete, and they now also pay us every month as well. We have also set up another tribe in the very south of Greece, and only last month, we established one in the south of Italy.

Oh yes, Gomer, from Affreidg, had established tribes in the north of that country and Dana and the rest of the tribe were creating settlements all the way up the Danube. As soon as Dana began a new colony, she moved on upriver, allowing new settlers to leapfrog through the existing settlements to find their own."

Cessair listened intently but said nothing. She was sure such expansion was bound to cause trouble in the future. She was pleased to hear news of Gomer and immediately thought of Dana's people advancing up the Danube. Hatti's voice recaptured Cessair's attention.

"Your vessels can be resupplied from any of these 'our' countries, and they are always ready to welcome you, and they are expecting you. Oh yes, you can also use Sicily as we also have people there as well. Your tribes will always be our friends and allies, and we will always remember what you did for us; thank you."

Cessair was surprised at how far they had expanded in so few years but was thankful to have allies along so much of her intended route. She thanked Hatti and Matanni, who then left. As Matanni was leaving, he pointed at Cessair's tooth and said,

"If you ever see Dana again, please tell her that I miss her."

With those words, they were all gone, leaving Partholon alone with Cessair. A few minutes later, Bith, Banba, Ladra and Fintan all arrived as had been previously arranged. Cessair said,

"Well! We are ready to go. We have several friendly ports, so I suggest we do not overwhelm the ports with our large numbers. We should travel in three waves of six ships. On board, we will make our

final plans for the last leg, and then we will all travel together as a group from Sardinia."

Ladra spoke next,

"I have good, experienced pilots but not all of them know the way to Sardinia; I will ensure that at least two pilots in each wave do.

How will you keep everyone informed and involved with so many people?"

"I thought of that." Replied Cessair.

"I want my first ship to carry one woman from each tribe. They will each act as each tribe's representative. Another ship will have one man from each tribe. Both groups will devise a set of rules for the whole society. In Sardinia, we will agree on a common set of rules before we move on from there; we need at least in principle a set of fair rules that respect everyone."

Fintan spoke up, *"So two ships will be completely of one sex; there are exactly fifty tribes."*

"Good, they will have no distractions from their important task." Said Cessair and added,

"Fintan, Ladra and Bith, you will be with me at least until we reach Sardinia."

"Here we go again – Meroe all over again!" added Fintan.

Cessair again turned to Partholon,

"With all this trading going on, I am sure that there will be goods we can send back and sell. We could load ships with goods, and then Partholon, would you please help to prepare more tribes for the journey as we become ready for them?"

"I will, of course. I hope the new land will be fertile and bountiful to support you all. I pray that Tabiti will keep you all safe until we meet again." These were Partholon's final words, and the meeting was over.

There were celebrations that night, but everyone was too busy or apprehensive to enjoy them. There were so many last-minute little jobs to be done or friends to say goodbye to. Partholon had arranged for his people to load the animals and supplies on the ship all through the night so that the first wave of boats would be ready to sail at first light.

Cessair was standing on the deck before the sun rose the following morning. She was not alone. Everyone on the first six boats was waiting for the light to let them set sail. She thought of that first dawn when she started her journey, as she had just left Affreidg. Then when she looked back, she saw the Black Sea that had destroyed Affreidg; when she looked forward, she saw the future for her tribe. This time when she looked back, she saw the vibrant town she had created and named and had kept her tribe safe and well. Now she was leaving it. She turned around, and there in front of her was another great sea looking very dark, but this time it was ahead of her. She quietly prayed,

"Manandan, please keep us safe."

The shadows of Troy were taking shape and form as Ladra called for the ropes to the pier to be cast off, and they were on their way. A huge cheer went up that surprised everyone. It had been too dark to see the thousands of people present that early morning. Some had travelled for miles, many all night, just to see the departure of the famous Cessair and her fifty maidens. These tribe representatives that they all came to see were to be the parents at the birth of a new Affreidg.

Api was kind to them that day; a stiff breeze blew from the north, and the ships made great progress. Most of the passengers had never been to sea before, and many marvelled at how such a big ship could even float and travel across the sea so fast. Ladra was very pleased with their progress, but several times he had to slow down to ensure that all six ships kept within sight of each other. He knew these waters well and could tell Cessair stories about most of the islands they passed.

"There is Santorini in the distance. The tribe there are real experts in metalworking, and they are also excellent sailors. On one of their smaller islands, they have a hot area that even the rock bubbles and boils. Many people are terrified of this area because they say it is the home of a furious god."

Cessair's Hegira Resumes.

Said Ladra, and he went on,

"We have made great progress today, and it will be dark soon, so I think that we will shelter there tonight. They have a great place to stay, as they have a ring of islands with the sheltered sea in the middle."

News had already arrived in Santorini about Cessair's hegira, and as soon as the ships entered the enormous natural harbour, the local population was there to greet them. Cessair did not expect such a welcome but could not refuse the festivities offered by the Santorinians.

They had planned to leave at first light the following morning, and they did not even plan to disembark, but their hosts gave a sharp warning of strong winds in the wrong direction and rough seas for their onward journey. Ladra knew better than to question the islanders' advice. These islanders' knowledge of the ways of the sea was renowned throughout the Mediterranean and was not to be dismissed lightly.

Every ship had enough tents and utensils to set up a small travelling village quickly. It was expected that the boats would seek safe anchorage each time the seas became rough, and the passengers would wait on dry land until conditions at sea improved. Ladra had not planned on staying here, especially as they had made such significant progress throughout the day in excellent sailing conditions.

"Believe me," said Antonio, the islander, *"when the wind blows from the north, and the seaweed becomes wet, the seas will become great and dangerous."*

Faced with such local knowledge, Ladra gave the order to make camp. No sooner than the temporary village was set up, dozens of islanders came carrying gifts of food, wine, or wood for a fire. Soon music started, and tall tales were exchanged for most of the night.

Antonio started the evening in the company of Cessair, Fintan, Ladra and Banba. Antonio was also a sailor who loved to travel so he and Ladra quickly bonded over their shared love of the sea. After what seemed like an age of talk of storms, wrecks, and near misses, Cessair, Banba and Fintan sneaked off to the nearest tent with good music and lively company. Moreover, neither Antonio nor Ladra seemed to notice, nor the trio thought would they have cared; but they were very wrong to assume that.

Sure enough, the following day, the sea was very rough, and everyone was glad that they were on dry land. Antonio was right about the sea conditions, and he strutted around, proud that his predictions had been so accurate. His arrogant manner, however, did not stop him from being the perfect host. He took them to see how they extracted the metal from the earth. Fintan showed the greatest interest here, and he even suggested a few ideas on how to make the process more efficient. He picked up a few valuable tips that he would use in the future.

Antonio took them to see where the earth bubbled and boiled, but none of them liked the smell of rotten eggs that was all around them. He warned them to stay very close to him as a few people in the past had wandered off alone and fallen through a thin crust of the earth; the angry god consumed them – nobody wanted that!

Sometime later, after they had returned to their camp, Antonio said that he knew a captain that used to live in Santorini but now lives in Sardinia. He has seen the new land that Cessair was seeking and that he had been there many times. He said that the man had now stopped travelling.

He addressed Cessair and Ladra directly when he spoke the following cautionary words,

"In recent years, many bad men have taken to the sea. They attack defenceless small boats and steal from them. They sail away again and are never seen again. Be very careful and trust no one at sea. You need always to be prepared. An apparently damaged ship

that is crying out for help may have armed men hiding and waiting to attack your ship. Trust no one at sea!"

He repeated his warning and then continued,

"I know this captain well, as he taught me how to sail many years ago. He knows of many of the bad men and keeps bad company, but his knowledge would be of great use to you. I could go with you to Sardinia and introduce you to him if you like. He could tell you the best route to take and where to stay overnight. He will need paid - but not very much!"

Concluded Antonio. This left Cessair with a dilemma, should she trust this man who is associated with thieves and pirates? Should she pay money to such a man who prefers to keep lousy company in Sardinia rather than retire back to his homeland of Santorini? However, a little money spent now would definitely make their trip to the Endless Sea a lot safer – that is, if the old captain told the truth. Could that old captain be relied upon?

It was Antonio's recommendation and genuine kindness that swayed her in favour of bringing Antonio to Sardinia.

"Yes, please introduce me to this old sea captain in Sardinia."

Said Cessair as they returned to their temporary camp.

They broke camp before dawn and boarded the ships, ready for an early start. They hoped that Antonio's prediction of favourable winds would also prove right as it had the previous day. He was right again. They travelled fast and spent that night in a secluded cove in the very south of Thrace. The next night they stayed in a cove close to where the boot of Italy was about to kick Sicily! On the third day, they reached Sardinia just as the dark was falling, and again they stayed on board.

The following morning, they entered the busy port town. It was like no place that they had ever been to before. They were used to a busy seaside town having a pier and boats coming and going, but the dock was secondary to regular business everywhere else. The townsfolk usually worked in different trades not associated with boats as their primary source of income. Antonio explained why this port was different.

"This is a new town built entirely around boats, trade and now, pirates."

Cessair, Banba and Fintan looked at each other in alarm as Antonio continued.

"A sailor arrives and buys supplies or just wants to stay on land for a few days in friendly company. No one asks questions; they just take payment for the requested services, supplies, or damages caused. This town is full of dangerous people, but there is little crime. It is mostly tough men and women with too much to drink and many with lots of money to spend! The resident townsfolk just help them to spend it."

"I had heard of such a place, but I never considered it as true. It is said that anything can be bought here at a price." Said Ladra. *"Where does your old captain live?"*

"Here!" Said Antonio as he knocked on an old wooden door of a fine big house.

A young girl answered the door, and when Antonio explained whom they had come to see. She said.

"Come, grandfather is out the back. Please follow me."

The garden had large fig trees, and sitting under the shade of one of these trees was an old man with long bleached white hair framing a broad face. He had a face that had been well-weathered by the sea, a hard life, and the passing decades. A wide smile redrew the pattern of deep lines around his expressive face to one of joyous recognition.

"Antonio, my old friend, what brings you so far to visit me? Do you need more sailing lessons?"

The old man shakily rose to his feet when Antonio replied.

"Kallisti, these are my friends Cessair, Ladra and Fintan; they need your help and advice."

"Please sit, and we will talk." Said Kallisti.

They talked for hours, and Kallisti explained how he had seen a large island after sailing north in the Endless Sea for several days. The island was extremely fertile and green, and many large rivers flowed through it. The seas were full of many great fish, as were the rivers. He explained that he had landed there many times for fresh water and food, and every time there were plenty of small animals and fruits. The trees there grew much larger than any in the Mediterranean, and the grass was longer and greener than anywhere he had ever been before.

Cessair listened intently to everything that Kallisti said but what repeated over and over in her head was that this land seemed to abound in everything – a land of plenty. If this was indeed true, then she knew what she was going to call her new land.

As the day turned to night, Kallisti insisted that they should all stay as his guests, at least until the rest of Cessair's ships arrived. Cessair looked out, and high on a nearby hill was a great fire. She knew how quickly a large fire could spread in such a dry country, so she asked Kallisti.

"Do you see that large fire? Is it not very dangerous?"

Kallisti laughed and replied.

"We light that fire every night to help guide ships that arrive late in case they become lost in the dark. The fire is high up, so it

can be seen for many miles. The captains just head straight for it, and they arrive at our port. It has already saved many lives, and it draws passing ships to do business with our town."

Cessair could not make up her mind about Kallisti. He just kept doing good things but for the wrong reasons. The fire saved lives, but it was lit for more trade. He offered supplies to all sailors, including pirates; their 'blood money' was equally welcome as a bona fide trader's or even a pilgrim's alms. He did, however, know a great deal about this 'land of plenty' that she was heading for; therefore, whatever she thought of him, he was invaluable to her.

Kallisti, on the other hand, was taken by Cessair's drive and sense of purpose. He envied her youth, her opportunities, and those new discoveries that were just waiting for her before revealing themselves. He envied her naivety, her innocence, her ability to see beauty in nature unblemished by bad experience and cynicism. He thought hard before saying the following words.

"You will not be the first to land there. A group of people live on a small island just north of the main island. They cut stone and grind it into axe heads. These are the best axes I have ever seen; I have bought many of them and sold them at great profit across the Mediterranean. They have lived on this small island for many generations.

Sometimes fishermen from Iberia camp on your island, for weeks at a time, in the summertime before returning for winter. Your tribe will be the first to move as a tribe to the main island and make it your home. I wish I were a young man, for I would gladly have gone with you."

The following day Ladra spent many hours talking with Kallisti about the best route that the expedition should take. He mapped out all the refuge coves to look out for to stay overnight or if the weather turned bad. They even drew a rough map of the new land of plenty and some of its major rivers. Kallisti suggested a location that they should seek out as their first settlement. A place he had visited on several occasions when he needed shelter or supplies.

As dusk started to fall, Kallisti took his guests a short walk to a tall tower known as Nuralgi. They climbed the stairs that circled upwards, and there, at the top, was a platform for people to stand on. Once up there, the view of the sea was spectacular, and they could see for many miles. Ladra's keen eye spotted something on the horizon.

"Look!" He said, *"I can see our next six ships. They will be here soon."*

Kallisti complimented his remarkable vision and explained that someone was always up here, seeing who was coming to visit. They always wanted to be prepared, especially when a fleet of ships was on its way.

A few minutes later, Ladra spoke again.

"No, I was wrong; twelve ships are now coming together. The third batch must have made good time and caught up with the ones that left the day earlier."

"Good."

Said Cessair. *"Tomorrow, they can top up their supplies, and we will all leave the following morning."*

"So soon?"

Asked Kallisti. He was starting to enjoy the company.

The final push to 'The Land of Plenty.'

While the port was famous for its sea connections, the rest of the island made an excellent name for itself by producing fine-quality metals. Sardinia supplied vast quantities of copper artefacts to the thriving Egyptians and emerging countries all around the Mediterranean. In turn, Sardinia became an essential stop for the Phoenician traders.

The local population was known as the Sherden, and everyone sought their skills. Both Fintan and Antonio took the opportunity to meet with the metal workers, exchange ideas and processes, and exchange promises of working together in the future. As they were about to leave, the Sherden leader gave Fintan a gift of a pile of small dishes of highly polished metal; they were to be used on their dangerous journey ahead.

Cessair spent much of the day meeting with the newly arrived boats. She also spent time listening to the ideas for the new rules that the new country should obey. Significant progress had been made, but there still was a great deal of work to be done before the new laws could be considered ready.

Ladra called together all of the captains and gave them their orders for the rest of the journey.

"We will travel as one big fleet. Once we leave, we will travel towards the setting sun until we see land. We will follow the coast until we reach the Endless Sea. Then while staying well out to sea, we must always be able to see the land. The sea flow will take us north to our destination if we do this. If we go too far out to sea, the sea will take us south and draw us even further out into the Endless Sea, and we will be lost. If you cannot control your boat or cannot keep up, then rope your boat to one or more that can."

The final push to 'The Land of Plenty.

The meeting was just finishing when Fintan and Antonio arrived with the Sherden gift of the metal dishes. Fintan had no idea how they would be used and did not want to appear as stupid in front of everyone. Seeing Fintan's discomfort, Antonio addressed the meeting.

"These are to help you talk to each other while you are at sea. These dishes are so shiny that you can see your faces in them. If you reflect the sunlight into the eyes of someone on a ship even many miles away – they will see the flash and know that you want them. This is what the Sherden sailors do."

Each captain was given a dish and instructions on how and when to use it. They were all pleased with this new technology that was so much more efficient than shouting or waving.

Antonio was going to stay with Kallisti for a while and then he would find a ride back to Santorini, in a few months or maybe in a year or so. There was much work for him here as business was booming and many trading relationships were to be made.

Both Antonio and Kallisti refused any form of payment for their services, but Antonio added.

"Please let us be your agents here in Sardinia and Santorini if you want to trade with us. We know that you will have many things that we can use – Kallisti has seen some of them already!"

The sun was just rising when they left the port the following morning. The port was sheltered, and the wind had not yet picked up, so the ships had to be slowly rowed out. It was slow progress at first until they started to reach open water. They passed close by three large vessels that had arrived late the night before and had been anchored, waiting for daylight to dock at the port. As they passed close by, Cessair noticed the crews were rough and that they were armed to the teeth.

"What a dangerous lot. They are certainly up to no good."

She thought, and then she said to Ladra.

"Look at those dark ships; they look dangerous."

"Yes; they are pirate ships for certain"

He replied.

"We will avoid them at all costs if we see them at sea."

Then Cessair saw a face she recognised, and she felt sick, and her face went pale. She had a deep foreboding and knew that there was serious trouble ahead of them. Ladra saw her and became alarmed as he asked,

"Are you ok? What did you see? Shall we turn back?"

"No! It was not what I saw. It was whom I saw!"

Her weak reply was followed a few seconds later by a single name.

"Balor!"

They reached open water, and a stiff easterly breeze filled their sails, and they were all on their way at a fast pace. Antonio's last weather prediction was again proved to be correct, and they made good progress. All eighteen ships together made a powerful impression on the two boats approaching them. Ladra recognised them as Hatti's; they were setting up yet another colony, this time in the south of Iberia.

Three days later, they were ready to move into the Endless Sea. As soon as they passed through the Pillars of Hercules, everybody knew that they were travelling on very different waters. They had become used to the waves in the Mediterranean; they were smaller and more frequent. The waves in the Endless Sea were much larger and further apart. By looking at the other ships, even those quite close, it appeared that at times they were almost under the water and a few seconds later above it. On board, when a wave approached, the ship would rise and slow right down until it appeared to stop and then as the wave passed, the ship would career down the back of the wave at great speed. A few seconds later, the whole cycle started again. At first, most people were scared to see the next wave ahead and above them, but after a few hours, they became used to it.

They travelled north for a further three days until the land on their right ended, so they turned and went east. The wind was now behind them, and their progress had speeded up. During the third day travelling east, there was, once again, land ahead of them, and so as Kallisti had told them, they again turned north and followed the coast for an additional four days. When the coastline again turned east, Ladra knew he had to follow it until he could see land on his left side. It would be a long way out to sea in the far distance, but when he saw it, he should head for it. This land was close to where they were going, but it was already inhabited. Once they were close, they had to go west and follow the coast until, again, there was land on the left.

Nine days after they left Iberia, a shout went up.

"Land ahead!

There was great excitement and anticipation for the last few hours as their new home loomed closer and closer. Ladra was relieved to see the broad sheltered estuary ahead of them. The ships had taken a battering in the large waves, and even though they had stopped to rest several times, everyone was tired of travelling and everyone needed to rest.

They followed the broad river inland for a short distance until they saw a smaller river with a large island in its middle. This was a safe place to land; the island could be secured, and it would be easily defended. As the boats docked alongside the island, there were cheers, yells, and excitement. The land had never had so many people arrive together, and for the first time in its history, it was being settled.

Cessair, Fintan, Ladra and Bith reached the land together, closely followed by Banba and the rest of the fifty maidens on the lead boat; hand in hand, they came ashore. They all knew that they together were starting a new history for their race.

When everyone had landed and gathered together, Cessair addressed the crowd.

The final push to 'The Land of Plenty.

"Tabiti has safely brought us to this land of abundance or plenty. Manandan truly is a benevolent god; he brought our ships and us to safety in Dûn na m-Barc. Api is all around us; even the animals are not afraid of us and welcome us with their presence. The rivers and sea are full of fish, and the land is fertile and green. We are truly blessed, and I name this country after our goddess of plenty. Our home is to be called - Ériu.

A huge cheer went up as a great nation was born, and its name and stories would be repeated for millennia to come. These stories would be recorded and in time would, amongst others, become known as the Chronicles of Ériu.

Fini Volume 2.

Postscript.

Postscript Volume Two.

In this second volume, it might be useful to explain some of the history behind the themes. Again, the primary source was Lebor Gabála Érenn, as published by the Irish Texts Society.

Cessair was the daughter of Bith; Bith translates as "life," "world," or "universe." Fintan was the son of Brochna; Brochna translates as "ocean." These two are the cosmogonic couple that gave birth to Irish history. The concept of life, human society and social and commercial intercourse all coming to Ireland from the ocean is a theme repeated, over the millennia, until the arrival of men like St. Patrick.

Irish history was modified and often rewritten by successive conquering invaders. These invaders came with soldiers and violence or, in other cases, with business or diverse doctrines. The flavour of Christianity, as interpreted by St. Augustine and introduced by people like St. Patrick, needed to undermine and denigrate not only the humanity of pre-Christian Ireland society but also the already well-established flavour of Christianity. This had been introduced by the Apostle James several centuries earlier than St. Augustine's influence.

The very early Irish historians reported an Irish genesis that was instigated by Cessair, fleeing a great flood millennia before the Christian story. This flood was, perhaps, a folk rendering of the newly rediscovered flooding that created the Black Sea 7600 years ago. DNA evidence is now starting to support such a migration theory, at that time, of farming communities displacing the hunter-gatherer tribes in North-western Europe. The Irish DNA displays a difference between their farming roots compared to the hunter-gatherer roots of the neighbouring island that includes England.

The Lebor Gabála Érenn goes into great depth about the Cessair story and includes her 7¼ years of travelling and her sojourn in Egypt. Many of the references to Scotia in the Irish work may refer to two individuals with the same name generations apart but sharing a common background.

Plot disclosure spoiler, Scotia did marry Nel, and their descendants renamed Ériu's people as Scot – see later volumes. In later years the Irish successfully passed on this name along with the bagpipes to the country that now calls itself, Scotland.

Saball was referenced as Cessair's foster parent but the close connection between Scotia and Cessair in Egypt is my interpretation of the many close connections between Ireland and Egypt at that time. Some early Irish manuscripts do make the connection between Nel, Scotia and Moses.

References to many of the early Mediterranean tribes and their expertise are taken from many differing sources. The growth of the Hittite, Greek and Egyptian empires owe more to the growth of trade among those super-powers than many earlier historians have heretofore given credence.

Sea travel also became critical in the history of Mediterranean countries, but this factor was completely underestimated by the juggernaut superpowers of the day. This was an underestimation that in later generations, in around 1200 BCE, all of the land-based superpowers would regret greatly – again, see later volumes.

Postscript.

Author's Synopsis of the Chronicles of Ériu Series.

I published this series to offer a plausible historical backdrop for the first colonisers of Ireland. It introduces Cessair, the original settler who worked in harmony with nature, Partholon an exploiting businessman, Phoenician sea traders, Fomorian sea-pirates, The FirBolg or Bag Men, The Tuathe de Danan, the Druids or magic people, and the Milesians the descendants of Scotia the daughter of an Egyptian Pharoah, plus many others as the series progresses.

These books are published to inspire an interest in investigating what really happened to the people on the island of Ireland since the Ice Age. I have drawn evidence from ancient texts and associated commentaries. I have added the latest scientific findings and analysis to construct a plausible history that is free of political bias.

Successive conquering invaders have written Ireland's popular history for many centuries. It has been written to glorify and justify their reasons as to why Ireland was invaded by them rather than face many uncomfortable truths. Truths such as the enforced annulment of equal status and power of women. Equality and respect had been enshrined in Irish Brehon law from the earliest of times.

The series starts with the flooding of a vast area of highly fertile land 7600 years ago; this area is now known as 'The Black Sea.' It follows the stories of characters named in the ancient Irish texts that forged Ireland. It describes how the farming and metalworking Irish stood well apart from the rest of the hunter-gatherers in Northern Europe and how, instead, they had close ties with the Eastern Mediterranean and Egypt via the then very active sea routes.

The series also covers the collapse of the Mediterranean civilisation at the end of the Bronze Age. Later volumes show how Ireland led 'The Britons' to be the first area in the world to declare itself Christian in AD 250, well before Rome and two centuries before St. Patrick arrived.